Born in Lincolnshire in 1912, Michael Francis Gilbert was educated in Sussex before entering the University of London where he gained an LL B with honours in 1937.

He joined the Royal Horse Artillery during World War II, and served in Europe and North Africa, where he was captured and imprisoned – an experience recalled in Death in Captivity. After the war he worked in a law firm as a solicitor, and in 1952 he became partner.

Gilbert was a founding member of the British Crime Writers Association, and in 1988 was named a *Grand Master* by the Mystery Writers of America – an achievement many thought long overdue. He won the *Life Achievement Anthony Award* at the 1990 Boucheron in London, and in 1980 was made a Commander of the Order of the British Empire. Gilbert made his debut in 1947 with *Close Quarters*, and has become recognized as one of the most versatile British mystery writers.

MICHAEL
GILBERT

STAY OF EXECUTION

HOUSE OF
STRATUS

This edition published in 2011 by House of Stratus, an imprint of Stratus Books Ltd., Lisandra House, Fore Street, Looe, Cornwall, PL13 1AD, U.K.

www.houseofstratus.com

Typeset by House of Stratus.

A catalogue record for this book is available from the British Library and the Library of Congress.

ISBN 0-7551-0533-8

Preface

The stories in this book cover a period of twenty-one years, which is almost exactly the span of my own legal practice. In re-reading them, and, in a few cases, making the emendations suggested by the passage of time, I have been struck by two things.

The first was a sad reflection that nearly half of the periodicals and newspapers in which these stories originally appeared have now disappeared from the scene. I could not believe that their demise was solely attributable to my contributions, and I was puzzled to account, as many people must have been, for the practical disappearance from the bookstalls of that old favourite, the short story magazine. Where are the *Strand* and the *Grand* and the *Windsor* of yesteryear?

One theory is that people nowadays have got so mentally conditioned that they prefer their entertainment to be entirely predigested. Before they will accept a story, someone has to turn it into a sequence of scenes, have the scenes enacted, and photographed, and then transmitted on to a screen. Instant entertainment, to be absorbed with your instant coffee. I think this is over-facile. I fear that the explanation is not that people read less. In fact, they read more, but they read different things. It is the enormous growth of the paperback which has wiped out the short story magazine. The long-distance train traveller, who used to be the staple purchaser of magazines, can now buy, for much the same price, a complete book by his favourite author. And he buys it.

This development may have been inevitable, but it is particularly sad in the field of the detective or crime short story. As writers have shown, from Conan Doyle and G. K. Chesterton to Raymond

Chandler and Roy Vickers, a short story of anything from five to fifteen thousand words is the ideal vehicle for a work of this genre. The best detective stories are built round a single idea: a novel method of murder, a subtle motive, an ingenious alibi. They are essentially artificial constructions (but so were the ballade and the sonnet). What ruins them most surely is when they are dragged out, artificially extended to eighty thousand words, with plans of the scene of the crime and lists of who did what, where. An example of this was H. C. Bailey, whose short 'Mr. Fortune' stories are small masterpieces, but whose full-length novels, about the same character, are sadly hard to read.

The second thought which occurred to me was how little, in essentials, the law had changed in this period of time. 'Black market offences' has an old-fashioned ring nowadays, and when *Stay of Execution* was written, it was still possible, though uncommon, to be hanged for murder. But the essentials of legal theory and practice are curiously stable in an unstable society; the law of contract, which governs the agreements we make and forces everyone (except trade unions) to honour them; the law of tort, which prevents us being an intolerable nuisance to our neighbours; the rules of procedure and evidence, which continue to make a trial in an English court the fairest which any accused can hope to get, and which are only sniped at by people who have not witnessed or experienced the proceedings of foreign tribunals. I am glad that it should be so. The Englishman's respect for the law (not, I hasten to add, for lawyers, who are regarded with feelings which range from dislike to tolerant amusement) is a life-line in the very stormy seas which are breaking over the seventies. I hope it will never snap.

Having said which, I have only to add, as I hope will be apparent, that none of the lawyers in this collection is real, and that none of them is me.

MICHAEL GILBERT

Back on the Shelf

During the war a lot of matters had to be put on one side. I should explain, perhaps, that I mean legal matters. I am the senior partner in – well, no. On second thoughts I'd better not mention names.

I'd better say that I'm senior partner in a very old and very well-known firm of City solicitors: have been ever since Herbert died, and that was twelve years ago.

During the war, as I said, things had to take their turn. Like everyone else we were understaffed and overworked and what with the disorganisation to start with and the buzz bombs towards the end, it was a standing miracle, to my mind, that anything got done at all.

When our young men came back from the war it took them some time to pick up the threads. You don't make – or remake – a practising solicitor in a couple of months, nor even in a couple of years.

But lately, gradually, the arrears have been getting worked off and one or two files have been brought into the light that I for one never expected to see again this side of doomsday.

I must confess to a certain sinking of the heart when young Bob, who is the most confoundedly energetic of the lot, came into my room one morning with a dog-eared folder, pale from the sunless depths of the second basement, and said, "I've been looking at Mrs. Oliphant deceased."

"If you've time to do that," I said, "I shall have to look you out some more work. Why, she's been dead for thirteen years."

"It wasn't her, exactly, sir. I was tidying up Charlie Fanshawe's reversionary interests – you remember, he was killed in North Africa, but some of his mother's estate only fell in last year – and I thought

1

I'd have a look at that money he got from his uncle—"

"Great-uncle," I said automatically.

"Yes, sir. Old Robert Fanshawe. I took a copy of his will home last night with me. Really, sir – I don't know if you remember it – it practically seemed to me to add up to nothing more nor less than an open invitation to murder."

"Good heavens," I said, considerably startled. "Look here. I can see you're bursting to explain all this. Jump into my taxi with me and come round to the club, and you shall talk about it over lunch."

"Robert Fanshawe," I said, when we had settled what we were going to eat – a most important thing to a man of my age. "Let me see, yes – rather an odd character. But his wife, if I remember, was odd as well. A pioneer of the cold water and raw carrot school of health faddists."

"Yes, sir, I gather her husband didn't see eye to eye—"

"He twisted his wife's tail about it, didn't he, in his will?"

"A most extraordinary document, sir. Home-made, I'm sure. Here – I've written down the bit that matters. His trustees are to accumulate all income for twenty-one years. At the end of that time, *but not before*, the whole lot, capital and accumulated income, was to be paid to the United Chlorophyllists – that's that health society his wife belonged to – provided that during those twenty-one years his wife had remained a member of the society, adhered strictly to its rules, and managed to stay alive.

"If either she, or the society, failed to survive the twenty-one-year period, then everything went to his nephew, Charlie Fanshawe."

"Yes," I said, "I remember him explaining that clause to me. You wouldn't appreciate it without understanding Robert Fanshawe. He was a late Victorian survival. 'Let her earn the money for her demmed society,' he said to me. 'If she can survive twenty-one years of their nonsense, I'm willing to believe there may be something in it. Otherwise the money's to go to young Charlie. He's only two now, but I can see he's going to enjoy a beef steak and a pint of beer when he grows up.'"

"No doubt, sir," said Bob. "It would have been quite all right if the trustees *had* accumulated the income.

"But so far as I can see they seem to have assumed that Mrs. Fanshawe was going to die before the twenty-one years were out – she was already sixty-five when her husband died – and they treated Charles as a sort of heir presumptive.

"Most of the income was spent on his upbringing, and they even advanced him lump sums from time to time—"

"He was an infernally fetching young man," I said. "His great-uncle was quite right about him. Let me see now – the trustees were my late partner, Herbert Overstrand, and the boy's mother."

"It's the trustees I was thinking about," said Robert ominously. "Charles's mother died in 1933 and for two years your late partner seems to have acted alone.

"By 1935 he must have realised his position. Why, old Mrs. Fanshawe had only to live for a further two years and the United Chlorophyllists – or their solicitors – would have been clamouring for their money.

"Not only the capital wrongly advanced to young Charles, but all the income ever spent on him. I've made a rough computation – at compound interest it came to nearly ten thousand pounds."

"As much as that?" I said. "That wouldn't have been a laughing matter for Herbert, would it? I seem to remember that he appointed another trustee about then to act with him."

"Yes, sir. And here I suggest is where we meet the villain of the piece. Mr. A. B. Smith."

"Villain!" I said. "Good heavens, do you think—? Here, have a little more of this smoked salmon. Don't forget to squeeze plenty of lemon over it; it brings out the flavour."

"Perhaps villain is a strong word, sir. But I do feel that his influence over your partner – however, let me go on.

"This Mr. Smith seems to have been rather an elusive person. I cannot find that anyone ever actually met him. Documents were sent to him at a *poste restante* address, and came back in due course, duly signed."

"As long as he sent 'em back promptly," I said. "Most trustees who live in the country are so infernally slow."

"Yes, sir. He seems to have been quite businesslike. It was at that time that they started having a quarterly doctor's report on old Mrs. Fanshawe. I'm afraid they weren't very encouraging reports – from the trustees' point of view, I mean. Apart from an occasional head cold, she seems to have been in robust health."

"Fresh water and carrots," I suggested. "There might be something in it after all. As a matter of fact, however, I seem to remember that it came out all right in the end. She passed away a week or two short of the end of the twenty-one-year period. So the money went to Charlie—"

"Yes, sir."

"I don't suppose he complained about having had some of it before he was strictly entitled to it. Anyway, he's dead himself now – he did very well in the war, you know. Stopped a shell splinter the day before Tobruk was relieved—"

I saw that Robert was looking embarrassed.

"It wasn't Charlie I was thinking about exactly, sir," he said. "After all, he hardly stood to lose. It was the trustees."

"The trustees?"

"Did you know that they visited old Mrs. Fanshawe on the afternoon of the day she died? They were with her for about half an hour. Her maid found her that evening."

"Heart failure," I said.

"Yes," said Robert. "At eighty-six I don't suppose there's much difference between heart failure and a bolster over the face – particularly if nobody is looking for it."

"You'll have to be careful, you know," I said, "saying things like that. People might take you seriously. Anyway, how do you know they were down there that afternoon. I don't remember anything being mentioned—"

"I found it in your partner's expense book for that day," said Robert. "'Fares to Dorking and return: self and co-trustee.'"

"Good heavens," I said. "How – how methodical. Do try some of this Stilton. Is there anything else in support of your theory?

Anything—er—concrete?"

"I don't know, sir." Robert looked distinctly unhappy. "I was going through some of Mr. Overstrand's own papers and I found this. It was with his other private papers." He produced a white envelope. Typed on the outside were the words: "To be opened only on the death of the last to die of myself and A. B. Smith."

"It looked, sir—I thought—do you think it might be something in the nature of a confession? He might have wanted to get the thing off his chest, and yet not to hurt anyone by doing so."

"You won't mind my saying," I said, "that it all seems a little far-fetched. You've been reading too many detective stories.

"Anyway, we can't open this until we have proof of Smith's death – and as you say, he seems to be rather an elusive person. In all my years at the office I honestly can't remember meeting him. Good heavens. Look at the time. We must be getting back."

In the cab I said, "It wasn't only to talk about the Fanshawes that I asked you out to lunch, Bob. You almost put it out of my head. Old Horniman wrote to me last week that he's looking for a junior partner and he was kind enough to offer me first nomination from my firm. I must say, I had no hesitation in putting forward your name, and I heard this morning—"

The remainder of the drive back to the office was occupied with Robert's thanks and my disclaimers of them.

"It's a good opportunity," I said, "but I think you're the man for it. You've shown that you possess an enquiring mind and plenty of persistence, and that's what a solicitor needs."

Back at the office I said, "By the way. I don't think we ought to leave that file lying about. Put it back where it came from. I'll get your successor busy on it some time. And you might put that envelope safely back in the Overstrand box."

I didn't tell him, of course, that it was empty or that I had long ago destroyed Herbert's maudlin 'confession'.

Ha! I didn't tell him who A. B. Smith was, either.

The Blackmailing of Mr. Justice Ball

"So Popsy is dead at last," said Mr. Rumbold. "Extreme senility, coupled with fits. Excellent!"

It was the habit of the senior partner in the firm of Wragg and Rumbold (Solicitors of Coleman Street), to open his post every morning with the assistance of his senior managing clerk, Mr. Silverlight. The two old gentlemen had joined the firm on the same day in the early Thirties, Mr. Rumbold as an articled clerk, Mr. Silverlight as a post room boy.

"Well, well, well," said Mr. Silverlight. "That is indeed a blessing."

"Topsy was run over two years ago, wasn't she?"

"At her age, she shouldn't have been in the road at all."

"And that's the end of them all."

"It's the end of a chapter," said Mr. Silverlight.

And so it was, thought Mr. Rumbold. The end of a long chapter, a chapter which had started nearly twenty years before, when Miss Manciple had come in to make her will. He could see her now, sitting in the very chair occupied by Mr. Silverlight, her hands clasped over the silver knob of a black ebony walking-stick, her light grey, very slightly mad, eyes fixed disconcertingly on him.

Her instructions, however, were perfectly clear.

"I have no direct descendants," she said. "The closest members of my family are my nephew, Norman, and my niece, Venetia. And when I say they are my closest relatives, I must add, Mr. Rumbold, that neither of them has been all that close. A small gift at Christmas, a card on my birthday. Is that how your family treat you?"

"I'm lucky if they remember my birthday," said Mr. Rumbold. "But pray proceed."

"My most constant and faithful companion for the last ten years has been my darling Siamese cat, Sunny. Mai Tsun is her official name, but she is always called Sunny. People will tell you that Siamese cats are aloof and unfriendly. It's a fallacy. They are extremely intelligent, far more so than most human beings. They have extra-sensory perception, and can communicate with each other over wide distances. But they are not proud about it. If you treat them as equals they are perfectly willing to reciprocate. After I go, our sole care must be for her."

"You mean you wish to leave her all your money?"

"Is that possible?"

"Well, no," said Mr. Rumbold, wishing that his clients would not constantly spring problems like this on him. "But what you could do is to direct that the income from your estate should be devoted to the upkeep of your present house as a home for Sunny, and to pay the wages of some suitable person to look after her. You have a companion?"

"Miss Tape, yes."

Mr. Rumbold remembered Miss Tape, a mouse-like creature who sometimes accompanied Miss Manciple on her jaunts up to London.

"Splendid," he said. "We will direct that she shall be allowed to live in the house, be paid a salary, and look after things. I take it that when Sunny finally dies—"

"Siamese cats do not die, Mr. Rumbold. Their souls travel onward, and upward, to a plane altogether higher than anything we can comprehend."

"When Sunny passes on," amended Mr. Rumbold adroitly, "I take it you would wish Miss Tape to have an annuity—"

"A small annuity. Her usefulness will by then be over."

"And subject to that, the estate then to go equally to Norman and Venetia—"

"What happens then," said Miss Manciple, "is a matter of indifference to me. Let me have the document to sign as soon as you can."

Mr. Rumbold had discussed the problem with Mr. Silverlight.

"I suppose we're not worried by the rule against perpetuities," said Mr. Silverlight. "Even if the first part isn't charitable, there's a gift over."

"Surely, we have a life in being—"

Mr. Silverlight looked doubtful. "I'd always understood that to mean a human life," he said. "Wasn't there a case where someone tried to settle a fund during the life span of a giant tortoise? It was overruled in the Court of Appeal."

"What we'll do," said Mr. Rumbold, "is to say that the income of the estate shall be devoted to paying the outgoings of the house and a salary of five hundred pounds a year to Miss Tape for a period of twenty-one years *or* the life span of the cat, Sunny, whichever is the shorter. That must be safe. A cat couldn't possibly live to be thirty-one, could it?"

"I don't think so," said Mr. Silverlight. "Who's going to be executor?"

"I am."

"There'll be trouble over this, you know."

"I'm afraid so," said Mr. Rumbold sadly.

"That nephew, Norman. He's not a very agreeable character. An insurance investigator, I believe."

"I've never met him. But I do remember the niece. She seemed a pleasant enough character."

"She's married a stockbroker. I don't think he's going to like it."

"Don't let's cross our bridges before we come to them," said Mr. Rumbold. "This blasted cat may die before Miss Manciple."

The trouble which Mr. Silverlight had anticipated took concrete form some three years later. The death of Miss Manciple was not unexpected. Shortly after executing her will and lodging it at her bank she had suffered the first of a number of slight strokes. For the last nine months, with her mind gradually failing, she had been confined to her bed, and her affairs had been looked after by Mr. Rumbold with the aid of a Power of Attorney.

What did cause surprise was the will itself. For Miss Manciple had altered it. Over the clause which contained the words, "During the lifetime of my Siamese cat, Sunny," she had inserted, in her crabbed but legible handwriting, the words, "And her legitimate offspring."

"We shall be in the Probate Court for certain," said Mr. Rumbold. He said it without pleasure. Like most solicitors, he regarded litigation as a nuisance, something which disrupted the routine of the office, which might come out well, but was equally likely to come out badly, and for which in either contingency a solicitor was inadequately remunerated.

"I hope we get a reasonable judge," said Mr. Silverlight. "I can think of one or two who are going to be pretty scathing about this will. Why on earth did we let her monkey about with it?"

"We had no say in the matter," said Mr. Rumbold. "She simply took it away, said she knew how to have it executed properly – which I must admit, she has done – and popped it into her bank. I haven't seen it from that day to this."

"Suppose we get Mr. Justice Ball," said Mr. Silverlight.

"I hope to God we don't," said Mr. Rumbold, and being a superstitious man, reached out to touch wood. His hand actually lighted on the base of his table lamp, which was made of plastic, and this may have accounted for the fact that when the case, *In re the Estate of Alice Manciple,* came in front of the Probate Division, it was set down in Mr. Justice Ball's list.

It is an undoubted fact that Mr. Rumbold's reactions to this news would, at that period in the late forties, have been shared by most practising solicitors. It is less easy to explain why. Mr. Justice Ball was an excellent lawyer and a man of iron integrity. In the days when such things were liable to happen to judges he would cheerfully have gone to the Tower, or even to the block, to uphold the independence of the Judiciary against the Crown. A bachelor, and a man of austere habits, his private life was a model to a laxer generation. If he had any weaknesses, they were professional rather than human. He was reputed to dislike solicitors. This was thought to arise from the fact that, as a young barrister, he had depended to a certain extent on their patronage, and, now that he was on the Bench, was not averse to getting a bit of his own back. He was also rather over-inclined, if he felt that Counsel were not doing the job properly, to conduct cases for himself, cross-examining the witnesses on both sides at greater length than the barrister who had been hired to do so.

Hargest Macrea Q.C. gazed round the crowded court, and reflected, not for the first time, that it was cases of no real legal significance, but of what the papers like to describe as 'human interest', which got all the real publicity. He was a tough and experienced advocate and had been selected by Mr. Rumbold as someone unlikely to be intimidated by the Judge.

"The facts in this case, my lord," he said, "are somewhat unusual. The deceased was a lady of strong character, and decided views. She was the possessor of a substantial fortune, and a freehold house at Much Hadham, where she lived, in comfortable circumstances, looked after by her companion, Miss Tape, and enjoying the company of a highly-bred female Siamese cat.

"These animals, as your Lordship may be aware, are exceptionally gifted creatures, and excellent companions for people of intelligence, being themselves endowed with almost supernatural powers of understanding and sympathy."

"You are preaching to the converted, Mr. Macrea," said the Judge. "I happen to be the owner of such an animal."

Macrea, who had, of course, been well aware of this, smiled politely. He said, "This particular cat was officially named Mai Tsun, but was familiarly known in the house as Sunny."

"When you say 'officially', you mean that this was the name under which she was registered in the records of the Siamese Cat Club?"

"That is so, my lord. These records showed that she was the offspring of a male cat, The Emperor Mu, and a female cat, Lady Lotus Flower. The records also identify the grandparents and the great-grandparents on the male and female side."

"Your object in this excursus into the genealogy of the animal, Mr. Macrea, is, I assume, designed to cover the expression '*legitimate* issue'?"

"Exactly, my lord. Miss Manciple's will has the effect, if I may use a lay expression, of tying up her estate for a period defined as 'the lifetime of my Siamese cat, Sunny, and of her legitimate offspring'. This has been interpreted by her executor to mean kittens born as the result of a regular union which would be recognised by the Siamese Cat Club. I should add that, shortly after the will was made, Sunny did give birth to a litter of six kittens, but since it was apparent, from their colour and other characteristics, that they were the result of a casual amour with a neighbouring marmalade-coloured tom-cat they were disregarded, and were in fact disposed of. However, at the end of last year, although by then of a very advanced age for child-bearing, Sunny was successfully mated with a pedigree Siamese cat, named Rampant Orchid, and produced four kittens, one male and three female. The deceased christened the eldest two Venetia and Norman, after her niece and nephew – the plaintiffs in this case – and the two younger ones Popsy and Topsy. It was thought right to have these kittens separately represented. My learned friend Mr. Kaye appears for them."

"And who is paying Mr. Kaye's fees, may I ask?"

"Being without any means of support, they were able to obtain assistance from the Legal Aid Fund."

Mr. Justice Ball said something under his breath, which, perhaps fortunately, the official reporter failed to catch. It was known that he did not approve of the recently promulgated Legal Aid and Advice Act.

"I will now call my instructing solicitor, Mr. Rumbold, who will prove the will."

Mr. Rumbold gave his evidence shortly, and was not cross-examined by Mr. Leopold, the barrister appearing for Norman and Venetia. The Judge, however, seemed unwilling to let him go. He said, "Am I to understand that you had no knowledge of this curious handwritten addition to the will you drew up?"

"That is so, my lord," said Mr. Rumbold, his heart sinking.

"And do your clients usually attempt to improve on your draughtsmanship?"

"It is very unusual."

"Did you not ask to see the will after it had been executed?"

"I asked Miss Manciple to return it to me, but she preferred to send it straight to her bank."

"Have you any idea why she should do so?"

"Possibly, my lord, she considered that I might be critical of her amendment."

"That would seem to argue a lack of confidence in her solicitor," said Mr. Justice Ball. Since this did not appear to be a question, Mr. Rumbold thought it wiser to say nothing, and the Judge, after peering at him over his spectacles with a look of loathing, dismissed him. Mr. Rumbold returned, fuming, to his seat.

The next witness was Miss Tape. After being told, several times, by the Judge to speak up she produced a reasonably clear account of life at Much Hadham.

The income of the estate had been sufficient to run the house, to keep Sunny, her four offspring, and Miss Tape in modest comfort. It was thought very unlikely that Sunny, now in her thirteenth year, could produce any further offspring, but the four kittens she had produced were all healthy, and might well live for twelve or even fifteen years more.

Mr. Leopold rose to cross-examine with an insinuating smile.

He said, "You would agree, would you not, Miss Tape, that twelve would have been an exceptional age for a cat to produce kittens."

"Oh yes. We were quite surprised."

"But did it happen, Miss Tape?"

Miss Tape looked startled. Macrea, rising swiftly to his feet, said, "I should point out, my lord, that this witness was not present when the kittens were born. This happy event took place in the presence of the local veterinary surgeon, who will be giving evidence later."

"My question has been misunderstood," said Mr. Leopold. "I am not suggesting that the four Siamese kittens, who are the third to the sixth defendants in this case, are not the legitimate offspring of a female Siamese cat. What I am suggesting is that they are not, and could not be, the offspring of the deceased's cat, Sunny."

"And why do you say it is impossible, Mr. Leopold?"

"Because, my lord, Sunny had died some months before the birth of these particular kittens."

Norman, whose investigations had unearthed this piece of

information a week earlier, grinned unpleasantly. Macrea turned a startled gaze on Mr. Rumbold and all the reporters raised their heads at once, and then, like a line of violinists obedient to the baton of the conductor, started to scribble in unison, 'Sensation in Court'.

"I take it, Mr. Leopold," said the Judge, "that you propose to produce some evidence in support of this startling assertion."

"Certainly," said Mr. Leopold. "If it should be necessary." He turned to Miss Tape, who seemed to be trying to conceal herself in the witness box, and said, "Is it not a fact, Miss Tape, that some four or five months before Miss Manciple died, Sunny herself succumbed to the onset of old age? And is it not also a fact that you approached a breeder of Siamese cats in the Midlands – a Mr. Carnworth – whom I shall call if I have to – and purchased from him an eight-year-old female cat, as closely resembling Sunny as possible, and substituted her for the deceased animal?"

It was not possible to hear whether Miss Tape said 'Yes' or 'No'. It is probable that she merely gulped.

"Are you suggesting," said Mr. Justice Ball, "that Miss Manciple, who was devotedly attached to her cat, would not have noticed the substitution at once?"

"Normally, my lord, I have no doubt she would have done. But you will recollect that she had suffered from a cumulative series of strokes, and her faculties were, by that time, seriously impaired. Also she was confined to her bed, and the animal was only permitted into her room for brief periods."

Mr. Justice Ball turned the full force of his very considerable personality upon the witness and said, "Is what Counsel suggests correct or is it not, Miss Tape?"

Whereupon Miss Tape had hysterics.

The Judge said, "I will adjourn the court until this witness feels able to resume."

The reporters raced for the nearest telephones.

When the court reassembled half an hour later, it was observed that Miss Tape was no longer in the box. Macrea, who had, in the interval, been doing some hard thinking and a certain amount of fast talking, rose to his feet.

He said, "I have discussed this development with learned Counsel on the other side, my lord, and he has agreed to my suggestion that we proceed on a basis that we agree that Miss Manciple's original pet, Sunny, did die at a date some months before her owner's death, and that the present incumbent – if I may so express it – is another cat called Sunny, who is the mother of the third to the sixth defendants."

"But if you concede this, Mr. Macrea, what is left of your case?"

"With respect, I must direct your Lordship's attention to the wording of the will. This says, 'During the lifetime of my Siamese cat, Sunny, and of her legitimate offspring'. In my submission this wording precisely covers the facts of the case as we now know them. The animal in question *was* a Siamese cat. It *was* known about the house by the name of Sunny, and it *did* belong to the deceased, having been very generously given to her by Miss Tape, to replace the previous animal. Her motive for concealing the substitution was the very understandable one that she did not wish to upset Miss Manciple during the closing months of her life."

"Even if this ingenious argument were accepted – and I feel sure that Mr. Leopold will have something to say about it—"

"Indeed, yes, my lord."

"—Even if it were accepted, is it not quite plain that the animal to which Miss Manciple intended to refer in her will was not the substitute – I should almost say, the impostor – which had taken her place—"

"I shall argue, my lord," said Macrea, "that it has long been accepted that this court will pay very little attention to what a testator imagines they mean in their will, and will confine themselves strictly to what the words say—"

When the court adjourned, Macrea said to Mr. Rumbold,

"Well, it was worth trying. But it's pretty clear that the Judge is hostile. I was surprised that he bothered to reserve judgment until tomorrow."

"I know exactly why he reserved judgment," said Mr. Rumbold.

"He has gone home to his bachelor apartment to spend a long and pleasant evening drafting a judgment that will be full of criticisms of the slovenly habits of solicitors, and may even go so far as to suggest that the whole thing was a plot, and that I was a party to it from the beginning. I wouldn't put it past him to award costs against me personally."

"I'm afraid you may be right," said Macrea.

But as it turned out, they were both wrong.

On the following morning Mr. Justice Ball kept his court waiting. This was unusual. He was normally punctual to the minute. When he did appear, it was evident that he was not himself. His eyes were bloodshot, and the dark shadows underneath them suggested that he had not slept well, if at all, on the previous night. He had also apparently cut himself whilst shaving, for there was a broad strip of sticking-plaster down the side of his jaw.

His judgment was short and to the point. He upheld the view that the reference in the will to 'my Siamese cat, Sunny' was equally apt as a description of the second cat, and that the relatives, therefore, would have to wait until the death of the last of the four kittens before claiming any share in the estate.

Even now, fifteen years later, Mr. Rumbold had no idea how this happy and entirely unexpected result had been achieved.

In wilder countries, in earlier and less civilised times, he might have supposed that severe pressures had been brought to bear upon Mr. Justice Ball; that he had been subjected to some form of intimidation or blackmail which, in the course of a single night, had forced him to change his mind. But in England, in that day and age, such an explanation was inconceivable. And even if it had been conceivable, the very last person who would have yielded to such pressure would certainly have been Mr. Justice Ball. The only other explanation which occurred to Mr. Rumbold was that he had had some form of stroke or brainstorm. But this had been conclusively disproved in the Judge's very next case, an exceedingly complicated affair dealing with Bills of

Exchange which he had handled with all his accustomed mastery; managing, in the course of it, to be rude to the solicitors on both sides.

"It's a mystery," said Mr. Rumbold.

Mr. Silverlight, who appeared to divine what he was thinking about, coughed discreetly. He said, "Previously I have never ventured to disclose something which was said to me, on that occasion, by Mr. Justice Ball's clerk, Mr. Henry. He and I were very old friends and he told me something, under the seal of strict secrecy. It may have had some bearing on the matter."

"Oh?" said Mr. Rumbold.

"Now that the last of the protagonists in the case is dead, I feel absolved from my undertaking. I cannot, of course, vouch for the truth of this. It is only what Mr. Henry told me."

"Go on," said Mr. Rumbold.

"Apparently when Mr. Justice Ball returned home that night, he was astonished not to be greeted, in the usual friendly fashion, by his own Siamese cat, a fine animal – I cannot recollect the name in the original Siamese, but in translation it was Cultivated Tigress. Not only did she fail to greet him. *She actually turned her back on him.* He was astounded. Such a thing had never occurred before. But worse was to follow. When he settled down after dinner to write his judgment – and you may surmise that it was *not* the judgment he eventually delivered – Cultivated Tigress came quietly into the room, and buried her claws in his ankle. By this time, he was thoroughly upset, and it occurred to him to ring up Mr. Henry, who was also a cat-lover. Mr. Henry was so alarmed that he hurried round. He found the Judge in a state of disarray and bleeding from a long scratch down the side of his jaw, incurred when he had incautiously tried to pick up and soothe his pet.

"It was then that Mr. Henry ventured to suggest that what they had encountered was an example of that extra-sensory perception for which Siamese cats were noted. The Judge at first pooh-poohed the idea, but Mr. Henry persuaded him to try an experiment. He said, 'Sit down, and start to rewrite your judgment in a manner favourable to Sunny and her offspring.' To humour his clerk, the Judge did so. The effect was electric and instantaneous. Cultivated Tigress became her own friendly self again—"

"Silverlight," said Mr. Rumbold sternly. "You're pulling my leg."

"On the contrary, I had the story from Mr. Henry, who witnessed it himself."

"Then he was pulling *your* leg," said Mr. Rumbold. "All the same," he added, "I feel glad that I have always stuck to bullterriers myself."

Murder by Jury

"Possibly you could describe the snake," said Counsel.

"Certainly. It was grey, a grey background with a mottling of red. Not crimson, darker than that. A sort of plum-coloured red."

"Yes."

"The underbelly, which was towards me, as it reared its head to strike, was also grey but lighter. Toning down almost to white in the centre."

"Was there anything else about it?"

"Yes – its size. It was as thick as two of my wrists together."

"I see. What happened next?"

"I seized it, just below its head, with both my hands together. My hands were turned inwards. I squeezed with my fingers and dug in my thumbs, and I felt the snake twist and squirm and batter its head from side to side as it tried to escape."

"And then?"

"Then I woke up. I was kneeling beside the bed. It was my wife's neck which was between my hands and her throat that I was squeezing. She was dead."

"That's an extract," said Chief Inspector Hazlerigg, "from the examination-in-chief of Edward Mason, on trial for the murder of his wife, Freda Mason. In my studied opinion he was one of the most thoughtful, cold-blooded, successful murderers we ever failed to hang."

"I read about it," I said.

18

"He got a lot of publicity," agreed Hazlerigg. "Acquitted murderers always do. It was my case, you know. And I can see, now, that I was outmanoeuvred from start to finish. In the very end, of course – however—"

(ii)

The case really started at six o'clock in the morning in the Caledonian Hotel at Chaffham-on-Sea, a small health resort on the Norfolk coast.

It started with a succession of loud screams from a bedroom on the first floor. 'Horrible and unforgettable' was how one witness described them.

The manager jumped from his bed, and, with one of the servants and two other guests, ran along to the room. The door was opened by Mr. Mason, who was apparently in a state of complete breakdown. He was in pyjamas, dishevelled and wild-looking, the pyjama jacket being torn. He kept staring at his hands and the only words he spoke, according to different accounts, were "I killed her" or "I strangled her."

The manager forced his way past into the room and found Mrs. Mason's body lying half in, half out of the bed. He sent for the police and a doctor.

When Mr. Mason was fit to talk he made a statement, and at no time afterwards did he substantially vary this statement at all. He said that he had had a dream. He was fighting with a large snake. He took the snake in his hands and throttled it. He woke up and found that he had strangled his wife. The dream was one which he had had before, but never with fatal results.

He added that he had loved his wife very dearly.

The local police could make nothing of this. Mr. Mason was not a local man. The fact that he had happened to kill his wife whilst staying at Chaffham was, they implied, entirely fortuitous. They handed the matter over, with some relief, to London and the case was given to Inspector Hazlerigg for consideration. A local coroner's jury returned an open verdict.

Hazlerigg disliked the case from the first. The essential information, as he appreciated, was locked up inside Mr. Mason's mind and provided he kept his head under cross-examination it was going to stay locked up.

"The way I look at it is this," said Hazlerigg. He was holding an off the record discussion with the Director of Public Prosecutions. "Supposing we had one of those hidden witnesses you read about – I've never struck one personally, but you know the sort of chap I mean – he's up on a cliff with a telescope and he happens to be looking in at the bedroom window. He sees Mason get out of bed, walk round, bend over the bed and strangle his wife. So what? What would it prove? How would we know if Mason was sleep-walking, or if he had all his wits about him?"

"I agree," said the Director of Public Prosecutions. "As it stands at the moment there's much less than a fifty-fifty chance of a conviction. If anything else turns up, well, we'll have to think again."

The next thing that turned up was Mrs. Mason's brother, Hector. He was a great big, hefty person, with a bull neck and hands like a pair of warming pans covered with red fur.

He said, "Did the police know that Mason had insured his wife's life for ten thousand pounds?"

Hazlerigg said, "Yes. That has come to light. In fact they had both insured each other's lives – not an uncommon arrangement with married people. Also the insurance was by no means recent. It was first taken out when they married and had been successively increased. The last increase – a big one, it was true, from five to ten thousand – had been made more than three years ago."

"If you'd known Ted Mason as I did," said the brother, "you'd have realised that that was just like him. A far-seeing, cold-blooded fish. And another thing – that business about loving his wife was the most arrant flap-jack. The two of them were hardly on speaking terms."

"Can you bring evidence of that?"

"Certainly," said the brother. "And plenty more. For instance, there was another woman." He gave details.

"The fact of the killing's undenied," said the brother. "There's your motive. If you don't prosecute I'll raise such merry hell in the press that you'll find a new commissioner at Scotland Yard before the year's out."

"The threat didn't bother us," said Hazlerigg. "Our hides are so thick by this time that little private darts like that don't stick. But when we put the new facts up to the D.P.P. he came down on the side of the prosecution. Indeed, it might be said that in fairness to Mason himself we could hardly *not* prosecute. There was a lot of talk going round. The thing had to be cleared up.

"I may say straightaway, that the evidence about the other woman turned out to be quite inconclusive. The brother swore that she was Mason's mistress. She swore that she had never even seen him.

"Macrea was defending when the case came up at the Central Criminal Court, and, my goodness, his handling of that brother was masterly. He went into the box looking like a cross between Bulldog Drummond and the Angel Gabriel and when he came out there was hardly enough left of him to cover a sixpence.

"Macrea took the obvious line, that he was a nasty-minded, prurient busybody, who had never liked his brother-in-law and had never lost any opportunity of blackening his character. How did he know about these alleged passages between his brother-in-law and this other woman? Had he been hiding behind the curtains? Or under the bed? And so on. The art of the thing was the way he got the chap admitting to the most absurd prejudices – he convicted him time and time again out of his own mouth.

"Nevertheless, making a fool out of a witness is a two-edged weapon, and when the prosecution closed I could set what was in the jury's mind as clearly as if they had said it out loud.

"'This chap Hector may be a fool,' they were thinking. 'He didn't show up too well in the box. But that doesn't mean that everything he said is untrue. There's no smoke without a fire. And there have been one or two other witnesses who gave evidence that things were not entirely happy between Mr. and Mrs. Mason. No open quarrels, but of course if Mason is the deep-dyed villain the prosecution are making him out to be, he would have taken good care to avoid open quarrels. Perhaps it isn't true about the other woman – we didn't much like that part of the evidence. But you can't argue away the insurance. Mason does stand to collect ten thousand pounds. If he *didn't* murder her, then undeniably she died as the result of an accident, and the insurance company will have to pay and look pretty. That's not disputed. But did he murder her? That's the simple point. Really when you get down to it, most of the evidence is practically irrelevant. That's the question we've got to answer. We are rather inclined to think that he may have done, but that, of course, is not enough. We'll have to wait and see how he shapes in the box.' "

Mason made an excellent witness.

He avoided the prime fault of a prisoner who gives evidence in his own defence – he did not protest too much.

He admitted small quarrels between himself and his wife. Married life, he said, was like that. You had differences of opinion, and you made them up. The jury appreciated that. A lot of them were married themselves.

He dealt fully with the question of life insurance. The total amount of the benefit, he said, depended on the premiums you could afford to pay. When he was beginning in business, and his earnings were increasing slowly, he had added gradually to the annual premium. Three or four years ago he had made rather large profits and had been able to double the premium. In recent troublesome times his earnings had dropped – he was an importer – and he had not therefore been able to add to the premiums at all. He had not reduced them, because that would have been uneconomical,

("You notice, incidentally," said Hazlerigg, "how neatly he gave them a point and then took it away again. The prosecution would certainly have elicited, in cross-examination, that he had recently been losing money and this would have constituted an extra motive for murder. By announcing the fact in advance he robbed it of half its sting.")

He denied flatly ever having seen or spoken to the other woman in the case.

Of the events which led up to the strangling of his wife he spoke calmly, almost objectively, without any undue display of emotion. He was always ready to give the fullest and most careful details and he never contradicted himself. And even so he avoided sounding too pat. He would remember some extra detail when questioned, or introduce some unimportant point, confessing that he had forgotten about it before. ("You can judge for yourself. I read you a bit of his evidence just now.") If it *was* lying, people couldn't help feeling that it was some of the most perfect and painstaking lying they had ever heard.

Even so, you could sense that the jury were still not quite happy about it.

Juries go more by instinct than people think. And as every additional fact pointed the other way, their instincts only told them more clearly that the man in the dock was a dangerous chap. Had they been forced to put their feelings into words the only sort of argument they could have put up was something like this: "The facts show that he did strangle her. He is plainly a quiet, controlled, sort of person – not, on the face of it, very likely to have nightmares and to run amok. We would like some positive evidence that what he says is true. That he did it in his sleep."

Looking back on it, in the light of after-knowledge, one can see that this was precisely the point which Mason wished them to reach. The timing of his defence was meticulous. First he erected this thin screen of doubt; then he proceeded to demolish it.

The next witness was his sister.

She was two years older than he was. A grey-haired woman, a middle-class intellectual and a good witness.

She started by recalling when she had slept with her brother – at a time when such a practice was respectable and indeed normal, their ages being ten and eight respectively.

She remembered very well the night when her brother had had a dream and had tried to strangle her. She did not think that the dream, on that occasion, had been about a snake. So far as she recollected the incident it had occurred on the night after they had visited a matinée performance of *Peter Pan*. Her brother had been very alarmed by the crocodile in the last act but one – the jury would probably remember it – and he had dreamed that the crocodile was chasing him. He had turned on her and got a good grip of her throat. He was a strong boy for eight and if nurse hadn't come running in she didn't like to think what might not have happened.

Cross-examination could make very little headway against this. She agreed that it was a long time ago, but an experience like that was not a thing which one was likely to forget. She particularly remembered it because from then on – until Edward finally went to boarding school – she had not been allowed to sleep in the same room with him.

You could see that the jury were shaken.

The next two witnesses completed the job.

The first – I won't give you her real name – we'll call her Lulu.

Macrea, introducing the witness, indicated that there might be passages in her evidence which would give offence, but plainly where life and death were involved, certain reticences had to go by the board.

Lulu proved to be pleasant and extremely self-possessed woman in her middle thirties. She was now leading a life of extreme rectitude, but she admitted – as the dullest member of the jury had by now appreciated – that she had at one time been a prostitute. She was giving her evidence of her own free will and because she couldn't stand by and see a man accused of something he obviously hadn't done.

Three or four years ago she had spent the night with the prisoner. It was the only time she had ever set eyes on him, but it was not an occasion she was likely to forget. At about six in the morning she had woken up to find him throttling her.

She was a strong and active woman and she had managed to fight her way free.

He had produced some garbled story about a dream and a snake, to which she had not paid much attention, being at the time both frightened and extremely angry.

The prisoner, however, had behaved very handsomely. He had given her ten pounds to soothe her feelings, and – more – had appeared so genuinely anxious and upset that she hadn't the heart to take the matter further. Her first intention had been to go to the police.

When Counsel for the Crown got up to cross-examine he found himself in a position of unexpected difficulty.

It is easy enough to throw ridicule on these poor women, and their evidence doesn't often count for a great deal in a court of law. But the fact of the matter was that she was plainly risking a wounding cross-examination with the inevitable unpleasant notoriety which must attend it with no possible motive except to save an innocent man.

In a way, you see, the more he hurt her, the less good did he do to his own case.

One must remember, too, that the witness had been sprung on him. Macrea had made it plain that the prisoner had been against her giving evidence at all. It was at her insistence, and because his advisers had thought it essential, that she had been allowed, at the last moment, to speak.

There was only one line that the prosecution could follow – and they hunted it for all it was worth. The whole story, they said, was a fabrication. It had never happened. The prisoner had simply purchased the testimony of this woman to bolster up his own defence. On the face of it, asked the prosecution, did the prisoner look the sort of man who could have had associations with a woman of this type?

Macrea must have grinned.

His next, and final witness was the doctor who had attended Lulu for bruises on her throat. He confirmed the date from his attendance diary. He also recognised the prisoner who had come with Lulu and settled the bill.

The jury acquitted without retiring.

(iii)

"And if I'd been on the jury I should have done the same," I said. "The man was innocent."

"He was guilty as hell," said Hazlerigg.

"Then the evidence was faked—"

"On the contrary. Every witness spoke the truth according to their

25

lights. So far as that goes, even Mason himself spoke the truth, about everything except the one vital point – what went on inside his own head."

"Are you asking me to believe," I said slowly, "that Mason was such a diabolical man that he started plotting the murder of his own wife at the age of *eight*?"

Hazlerigg put back his head and laughed heartily and at length. He rocked with laughter. Whilst he was laughing I began, dimly, to see the weakness in my argument.

"Now don't start blaming yourself," said Hazlerigg. "Because that's exactly what every member of the jury thought, in that instant when they acquitted him. After all, you can't expect all jurymen to be practising philosophers. If they had, they might have been acquainted with the dialectical trick known as deception by series."

"Explain."

"All right. I'll give you an example of the basic idea. Then when you want to plan your own murder you can work out the details for yourself. Supposing I have to deceive you about – say, the number of my house. For some reason it's not practical to alter the number plate itself. But I can take it down altogether or hide it. I lead you up the street, and point out that the two houses *before* you come to mine are numbered, respectively, two and four. You won't need much convincing, then about the number of my house, will you?"

"Six."

"So you might think. Actually my house is number four. I altered the number plate of the house on the left – which was really three."

When I'd worked this one out on the back of an envelope I said, "I think I see it. You mean that Mason—"

"When he decided to murder his wife, which was about three years before he actually did, he recalled the incident of himself and his sister. I have no doubt the story was perfectly true, though it may have become exaggerated a little with the passing of the years. Just the sort of thing any excitable little boy might have done. He knew that his sister remembered it, too. That gave him his true number, all he had to do then was to manufacture the false one. So he went out and picked up this woman – Lulu. He slept with her. In the early hours of the morning he started to strangle her. He didn't go very far, of course, just far enough to produce some convincing bruises on the throat. Then he quietened her down by paying her a good deal of money – I don't suppose she'd really have gone to the police, you know, they're shy birds – and he took her to a doctor and paid for the necessary medical attention. Incidentally, it was about the same time, did you notice, that he doubled his wife's insurance. Then he let three years go by. Then he strangled his wife."

"Knowing that any jury with those facts would acquit him."

"Yes. There was just one practical difficulty, and he surmounted that as well. His three witnesses were his sister, the doctor and Lulu. The sister he would always be able to get hold of. The doctor – even if he retired – would be in some medical directory or easily traceable. Even if he were dead, his records might have been looked up. The girl was different. They move, from time to time, and get swallowed up very easily in the whirlpool of the West End. If they retire, they take great care to sever all connections with their past. How was he to keep track of her unobtrusively? The method he adopted was to send her ten pounds a month, anonymously. He represented himself as some well-wisher who had received her favours in the past and wished to make this periodical contribution. So long as she kept him notified of any change of address, he would continue to send her the money."

"But if she had to notify him when she moved, surely she must have known who he was."

"No – the notification had to be sent to him at a *poste restante* under an assumed name."

"How long did it take you to find all this out?"

"Well, it took some weeks. We were only doing it to satisfy our own curiosity. But in the end we found the *poste restante* and the girl behind the counter gave us a definite identification. She picked Mason's photograph unhesitatingly out of a dozen others. He'd been calling for letters on and off for the last three years."

"Wasn't he running a considerable risk?" I said. "Supposing you'd got on to this before—"

"When the defence are allowed to spring last minute witnesses on you!" said Hazlerigg bitterly. "How do you think we were going to unearth all this in five minutes examination and cross-examination? That's why they kept Lulu up their sleeves until the last moment."

There did not seem to be a great deal to say. The story seemed to be without a moral.

"So you're absolutely certain that Mason did this murder, but you can do nothing at all about it. That's it, isn't it? You can't try him again, of course, for the same offence. He's safe."

"That's what he thought," said Hazlerigg. He was smiling, but his grey eyes had a far away look in them that I had learned to recognise.

"Some time later – more than a year after the trial – Mason was staying at a little hotel in Cornwall. He was still single. I never had much confidence in that story of the other woman. Even if it was true, he certainly never married her. He had a bedroom with a small balcony overlooking the cliff with a straight drop on to the rocks. The maid went to call him one morning, found the window unlatched and the balcony rail broken. What was left of Mason was among the rocks, fifty feet below."

"Then you were wrong," I said. "You were all wrong, from beginning to end. He did walk in his sleep."

"Possibly," said Hazlerigg. "Possibly. There was certainly no sign of foul play. One curious coincidence came to light later. Brother Hector had the room next door."

Xinia Florata

"I'm sorry to hear that," said Bohun. "When?"

"Last night," said the telephone.

"Peacefully, I hope," said Bohun. "Of course, it wasn't really unexpected, was it?"

The telephone agreed that it wasn't unexpected.

"He was – let me see – he would have been ninety this spring. That's a fine old age. Will you be wanting me to come down?"

In theory, when a valued client dies, the family solicitor always hurries to the house. In fact, there is little he can do that cannot be done, and better done, by the doctor, the vicar and the next of kin.

The telephone went on talking for quite a long time. Bohun listened, a tiny puzzled frown between his eyes.

"All right," he said, "I'll come along. But it looks as if what you really want is a competent police searcher."

Rowley Graine, his articled clerk, looked up, as a dog that hears the click of the front door. Outside in New Square, the trees and grass were green with spring.

"A trip into the country," he breathed.

"Yes," said Bohun. "Carshalton. It's old Tobias Buckley. He died last night. They've lost the will."

As they had the first class carriage to themselves Bohun filled in some background.

"The real tragedy of growing old," he said, "is that you lose things without realising it. Some people simply lose their wind and their waist-line. Others lose their wits."

Rowley, who was nineteen, said tolerantly, "I've got an aunt, sir,

29

who thinks she's a tortoise. She eats lettuce leaves off the edge of the table."

"Just concentrate on listening," said Bohun. "As I was about to add, Tobias was particularly lucky. He remained absolutely sane and just about as fit as anyone can be after four score years and ten in this vale. He kept fit by gardening and he kept sane by hanging on to his sense of humour. I don't mean that he played practical jokes. He'd got over that stage. His sense of humour had mellowed. It was of the quiet, reflective kind. Not the sort that appealed to Gertrude and Ambrose."

"The second cousins umpteen times removed who lived with him?"

"To be strictly accurate," said Bohun, "they were no sort of relative at all. They called themselves second cousins, but in fact they were just hangers-on. They've lived with, and on, Tobias for years, and I have no doubt that they hoped that if they hung on long enough he would leave them everything in his will. He was a bachelor, you see, and his mother and father were only children. They've long been dead, of course. His only brother died a bachelor too."

"Then," said Rowley, casting his mind back over the rules of intestate succession which he had been reading up only the week before, "unless they can find his will it looks as if the Grown will nab the lot. Was he well off?"

"Extremely well off."

"How very tiresome for Gertrude and Ambrose," said Rowley. "I bet they're turning the place upside down."

"I wouldn't be surprised," said Bohun.

When they arrived at The Retreat, a solidly unpretentious two-storey building with rather more garden than normal, they found a grim-faced Ambrose, a red-eyed Gertrude, and a house that looked as if it had suffered the attentions of a thorough-going gang of burglars and been hit by a tornado shortly afterwards.

They ate an impromptu lunch, laid on a hurriedly reassembled table (it had been turned upside down and its flaps unscrewed) sitting on chairs the seats of which had been removed, cut open, and roughly sewn together again.

"I think," said Bohun, surveying the battlefield, "that we may be approaching this from the wrong angle. To start with, do we know that he left a will?"

"I'm certain of it," said Gertrude. "You know that he had one before – I believe you made it—"

"I drew it up," agreed Bohun, "About six years ago. At the beginning of this year I was present when he revoked it by destroying it, in the presence of myself and my partner."

"I believe," suggested Ambrose, "that we benefited under that will."

"It may be so," said Bohun. "I forget the details. They can be of no importance now, surely?"

"Of course not, of course not," said Ambrose. "But he made another one. He wrote it out himself. He as good as told us so."

"When was that?"

"About ten days ago."

"Did he, though," said Bohun. "That's interesting. Did he say he had made it, or that he was going to make it? In fact, tell me exactly what he did say."

"It was after tea," said Ambrose. "He'd spent the afternoon in the garden. You know he was mad about gardening." Bohun thought he detected a certain pettishness in Ambrose's voice. Ambrose was not an outdoor type. "He'd finished digging that big bed the other side of the lawn." Ambrose went to the window and pointed. "He'd cleared out a lot of old stuff and was going to put in something or other else. I can't really think why he bothered. He'd quite enough money to pay for a dozen gardeners."

Bohun looked at the flower bed. It was the show bed of the garden – nearly eighty feet long and perhaps twenty feet deep, and tilted up slightly. When filled with flowers it must have looked theatrically beautiful.

"Did he do that?" said Bohun, surprised.

The bed was pitted with holes.

"No, no," said Ambrose. "*I* did that. I was telling you. He said to us, 'I hope you'll keep the garden nice when I'm gone.' I said, of course we would. I'm not keen on it myself but after all, we could always get

31

someone in. He then said, very seriously, 'If you keep the garden, you'll find that the garden will keep you.' He said that to both of us."

"It was perfectly obvious," said Gertrude. "Absolutely in character. He'd made his new will, sealed it up in a tin or something, and buried it in the garden."

"We used to do that with Easter eggs," said Rowley. He was disregarded.

"I see," said Bohun. "I gather, however, that you haven't found it yet?"

"It's a big garden," said Ambrose sadly. "We started on that bed, as it was the last one he was working on. Oh, here comes the vicar. And Dr. Plumb."

Two men were coming up the path from the gate. They were evidently familiar with the house, for they cut across the lawn, stopped to stare at the devastated flower bed, and then turned aside and came up to the French windows.

Ambrose let them in, a little sulkily, it seemed to Bohun.

After introductions had been effected, Dr. Plumb said explosively, "What in the world have you been doing to the garden?"

"As a matter of fact," said Ambrose, "I – that is to say, we – have been looking for something."

"Not found the will yet?" enquired the vicar. He sounded uncommonly cheerful, and it occurred to Bohun that neither of these old friends of Tobias Buckley liked Gertrude or Ambrose.

"It'll turn up," said Gertrude. "Is there anything we can do for you? If not, we happen to be rather busy—"

"Well—" said the vicar.

Bohun interrupted. "I wonder," he said, addressing himself to the doctor and the clergyman, "if you would mind stepping outside with me for a minute?"

Although he spoke with studied moderation there was something in his voice that brought all their heads up.

"Why – of course," said Dr. Plumb. "You'll excuse us?" said the vicar, preserving his manners. Gertrude nodded coldly. The three men walked across the lawn.

"What exactly," said Bohun, "was Tobias planning for this bed?"

"Not planning," said Dr. Plumb. "He'd carried it out. Not much chance of it coming up now, though. Looks like a battlefield."

"What was it?"

"Xinia florata. New type. Very neat, compact plant, with small leaves and a blue flower. Nurserymen use it sometimes for advertisement beds."

"Advertisement?"

"You know, 'Welcome to Smith and Brown's Nursery Garden', all done in flowers. That sort of thing. It's small, and a strong steady grower. As a matter of fact, you can write quite long sentences in it."

"Can you, though," said Bohun. "That's *extremely* interesting. Would you by any chance happen to know exactly what message Tobias had planted on that flower bed?"

"We don't know what the message was," said the vicar. "But it was something of sentimental interest, and it contained his name. We were there when he finished it. He drew his signature in the soil, and scattered in the seeds."

"And then—?" said Bohun, an unholy light in his eyes.

"Why then," said Dr. Plumb, "as we were his oldest friends, you know, he got us both to scratch our names, too, and fill them up with seed. It seemed a silly thing to do, but we would neither of us have wished to refuse. He was dying. I'd given him a month. We all knew he'd never live to see the flowers come up."

"And now," the vicar sounded quite unclerical in his anger, "those two – those two vandals – in their sordid greed for gold, have made quite certain that no one will ever see them. I doubt if a single seedling will survive."

Bohun stood swaying on his heels, looking dreamily at the scarred and pitted flowerbed. He agreed with the vicar. Tobias Buckley's last message would never now see the light.

"What a case it would have made," he said, at last. "It couldn't have stopped short of the House of Lords."

"What on earth?" said Dr. Plumb. "Why, good heavens—"

"His last Will and Testament. Planted in Xinia florata. Something quite simple. 'I leave everything to Gertrude and Ambrose'. Signed by him and his signature witnessed by the two of you. All in flowers. And then that precious pair had to dig it all up again. Oh dear, oh dear."

The three men were consumed with such wild and helpless laughter that Rowley came running, and even Gertrude and Ambrose stalked unwillingly out to see what the joke could be.

"If you keep the garden, the garden will keep you," said Bohun. It was hours later, and they were in the train, heading for London.

"Yes, sir," said Rowley. "But would it have been effective – a will made like that?"

"Good gracious," said Bohun. "I don't know. I'm just a solicitor. You know much more law than I do. Look it up in one of your books when you get back to the office."

Weekend at Wapentake

When Kilroy Martensen and his wife died in the Skyliner crash at Prestwick, it brought the family settlement to an end and gave Bohun a lot of work to do.

The memorandum came to light when he was searching through the old files. It was in a handwriting that he did not recognise, thin, rounded, not educated, not attractive, but extremely easy to read. "The Surviving Martensen of the last generation," it started baldly, "is Christabel; of this generation, Kilroy and Harriett, who are the only children of Christabel's late cousin Alastair. Under the settlement created by the will of Christabel's grandfather—"

And so on. It was a clear exposition of a complex set of facts. The man who had penned it had obviously been a sound lawyer with a certain talent for exposition.

"—Christabel enjoys the family property at Wapentake during her life. The house and estate is in first and second mortgage (see separate files) and would hardly clear these debts on realisation. The property is in a poor state of repair. The contents of the house, apart from the pictures and plate which are entailed, stand at Christabel's disposition. She lives alone, using part only of the house, with two servants, a married couple called Sherman. Mrs. Sherman appears to exercise a greater influence on Christabel than is really desirable. I am visiting Wapentake at the end of next week to talk to her on trust matters. I shall explain to her the disadvantages of dying intestate—" There the memorandum stopped. It was dated '12.x.48', and was the last paper on that file.

Bohun stared at the date for a moment, then went to the shelf and opened another fat wallet of papers. From it he extracted a Death Certificate. It stated that Christabel Drusilla Martensen had died, of cardiac distension, on the seventeenth day of October, 1948. Bohun clipped the memorandum and the Death Certificate together and carried them into the next room where his senior partner, Mr. Craine, lived.

"That's Sam Tucker's fist," said Tubby Craine, as soon as he spotted the paper. "I expect he wrote that just before he retired. He left us notes on all his clients. Not a qualified solicitor at all, you know. Started as an office boy with old Horniman, and worked his way up. Took night classes. People like that are the backbone of any law firm. You don't find them growing on every tree."

"This Christabel Martensen—"

"Of course, in theory he was only a managing clerk, but actually, in my time, he interviewed clients himself. And they were well advised to see him. Knew more law than any of us. I remember Martello – the old Duke, I mean, who was a bigger bastard than the present one, and that's saying something – wanted to raise money on his mother's reversion. Sam told him he couldn't do it. The old boy blew his top properly. When he'd finished shouting, Sam said, 'I've told you what the law is. You can hear it again from a High Court Judge if you prefer. It'll cost you a couple of thousand guineas, but I guarantee it'll be just the same law.' Marvellous, marvellous. No real offence, either. We still act for the Martellos."

"You notice that coincidence of dates," said Bohun, persevering. "He was going down at the end of next week. Christabel died suddenly on the seventeenth."

"How do you know it was sudden?"

"If she'd been ill when Tucker wrote that memorandum, surely he'd have mentioned it."

"I suppose so. I really don't remember. Look here, if anything turns on it, why don't you go and see Sam?"

"See him?" Bohun sounded slightly startled. "I imagined—"

"Good Lord, no. Right as rain. Nearly ninety, but going very strong. Lives at Streatham. I'll give him a ring and warn him to expect you."

Mr. Tucker lived in a neat, bright house on the exclusive side of Streatham Common. The middle-aged lady who opened the door said that she thought he was in the garden. He usually played clock-golf when the morning was fine. She deposited Bohun in the sitting room.

It was a cheerful room. The only outstanding piece of furniture was a towering, polished mahogany bookcase which must have been divided several times, laterally and transversely, to get it through the low door. Bohun strolled across to look at it and found that it was entirely filled with Law Reports – the old sets of Chancery and King's Bench which terminated in the year of Mr. Tucker's retirement – and a bound set of Law Reports which had been kept up to date, and clearly represented Mr. Tucker's current reading. There were no other books in the room.

When Mr. Tucker came hopping in, agile, spry, indestructible, Bohun realised at once that he was in the presence of a natural centenarian. He turned his mind to the Martensen family. The old fellow had no difficulty in recollecting them. His memory was as sharp as when he had quitted the office.

"Yes," he said. "I went down to Wapentake, just as I had planned to do. It was not quite the social visit I had anticipated, you understand. Christabel's sudden death put a stop to that. But there was a lot that could only be decided on the spot. Mr. Horniman was in Geneva. I was the only person available."

"You said 'sudden death'?"

"Oh, very," said Mr. Tucker. He looked at Bohun steadily for a moment, then added, "Most unexpected. She was seventy at the time, but in fair health as far as anyone knew."

"Cardiac distension," said Bohun. "I asked a doctor about it. It only really means that the heart stopped beating."

"Yes," said Mr. Tucker again. His head was tilted. He looked like a crafty old robin, uncertain whether to pick up an attractive crumb.

"Have you ever considered," he said unexpectedly, "how far old people put themselves into the power of their servants? Christabel was living quite alone. A mile in any direction from the nearest mortal. No telephone, even. She was substantially bedridden. Every moment of her day was governed by her servants, Mr. and Mrs. Sherman." He gave a disconcerting little laugh. "Well, if they were good, kind-hearted people, that was all right. If they were the contrary, consider their power. They prepared all her food. They helped her up and down stairs. They drove her in the pony-cart. They tucked her up at night. They could have killed her at their own convenience."

"If they had any reason to do so," said Bohun softly. "And were cleverer than the police. Who are quite clever men."

"Police?" said Mr. Tucker. "I don't underestimate the police. They are extremely effective in what I might perhaps call an arm's length murder. But what chance would they have in a cosy, domestic little tragedy of this sort? There were so many things the Shermans could do, or abstain from doing, that would kill an old woman of seventy. One pillow too many or too few. A wedged-open window on a foggy night. The wrong sort of food even, if they kept it up long enough. When things get serious, Miss Christabel wants the doctor. 'Yes, madam,' they say. 'He's coming as soon as he can. Tom's gone off in the trap to get him.' But of course they don't. Or not until it's just too late."

Bohun was listening with only half of his attention. With the other half he was trying to track down an echo. In the end he realised what it was. Mr. Tucker had spent so much of his life among legal documents that he had come to speak like them. 'Substantially bedridden', he said, and 'Do or abstain from doing'.

"Did you enjoy your visit?"

"It was the most remarkable weekend I have ever spent," said Mr. Tucker simply. "Do you know Wapentake?"

"I've seen pictures of it. It was a show place at one time, wasn't it?"

"I'm not a great hand at architecture," said Mr. Tucker. "It was too draughty for my taste." He looked affectionately round his own snug room. "All pillars and porticoes and arches of which someone had tired and had them bricked up."

"Blind arches," said Bohun. "I don't think they were ever meant to be used. Just ornaments."

"It may have been beautiful once. I should not like to state positively. It was after dark when I arrived. And then, so little of it was really being used. The two great wings had been shut for thirty years, and of the main part of the house only one corner was really lived in. It was like—" Mr. Tucker sought about him for the precise description. "It was like living in a box, inside another box, inside another box."

"Oil lamps and log fires, I suppose," said Bohun. He had a very clear picture of the little lawyer hopping down from the trap in the misty autumn dusk and advancing upon the huge, silent house.

"It wasn't uncomfortable," said Mr. Tucker. "As far as it went. I had a very nice dinner in the small dining room, sitting all alone at a table laid for eighteen. The Shermans waited. He was an odd character. White-haired with a sort of absent-minded distinction. You might have taken him for an Oxford don. It was only when you looked at his hair and finger-nails in a better light that you changed your mind. She was a terrible woman. Perhaps I'm being wise after the event, but I don't think so. Real, hard selfishness writes with an unmistakable pen on the human face. It can be oddly charming in the young. Not so as we come to middle age. She was a big woman, with a white face, and dressed in black. I can really tell you little more about her."

Bohun said that he now had a most accurate picture of Mrs. Sherman.

Mr. Tucker bowed fractionally as counsel do when the Judge commends their efforts.

"After dinner," he said, "Mr. Sherman went for the coffee and I apprehended that his wife wanted to talk business. I had no objection. For my taste the less time I had to spend there the better. She said, 'I understand that the heirs are cousins.'

"'Second cousins,' I said. 'Alastair Martensen's children.'

"'But it's only the settled property that goes to them.'

"'That is so. The house and land pass to them under the settlement.'

"'Little profit they'll get out of that,' she said.

"I must have looked my surprise, for she added rather defiantly, 'Miss Christabel had no secrets from us. We knew that the land and house and pictures and plate were tied up. But the rest of what's in the house, she could do what she liked with that.' She looked at me out of the corners of her eyes.

"'Yes,' I said. 'She could dispose of her free estate as she wished. But perhaps you'll excuse me saying,' I went on, for I was a little nettled, 'that it's no concern of yours.'

"'Indeed it concerns me – or us, rather,' said Mrs. Sherman, for her husband had come in with the coffee at that moment. 'All that she *could* leave she left to us.'

"I must have sat staring at her.

"She swept to the sideboard, picked up a paper she had put ready to hand and laid it before me. Then she went on with the clearing of the table, but with a sort of subdued and ferocious triumph.

"It was not a long paper, but I read it slowly, because I wanted time to think.

"The body of the document was in a strange handwriting, but well written and well phrased. As I looked at it my eye fell again on Mr. Sherman and I thought that perhaps my first guess had not been so far from the truth. Here was an educated man who had fallen on evil days. A school master, or possibly even that professor that my imagination had painted. I felt no doubt that his was the hand that had penned the document. I cannot now recall the precise terms, but its effect was clear and unambiguous. Christabel Martensen left everything that she could leave, including the entire contents of the house (these were specifically mentioned) to the pair of them in grateful recognition of their faithful services. And it was signed by Christabel. I had seen her vast disjointed signature too often to doubt it. Under what compulsion or misapprehension I could not guess, but she had signed it all right.

"I said, 'But you know, this isn't worth the paper it's written on.'

"Mrs. Sherman stopped clearing the table. She had the bread-board in one hand and the knife in the other and as she turned the light ran up the blade.

"'It's signed and witnessed,' she said, quite quiet.

"'You and your husband witnessed it,' I agreed. 'Unfortunately that means that neither of you can take any benefit under it.'

"'Is that the rule?' she said, and she took a slanting look at her husband, who stood there dumb.

"'I'm afraid so,' I said.

"I knew, then, as plainly as if they had told me, that they had done murder, and all for nothing. To break the long silence I said, 'I've changed my mind. I'll have coffee in the library.'

"Sherman picked up the tray and followed me in. Apart from the dining room the library was the only inhabited room on the ground floor. I fancy Christabel had used it as a sitting room. There was a fire of logs alight in the grate, but by that time I wanted somewhere where I could get my back up against a solid wall.

"'I'll sit there,' I said, pointing to a table in an alcove completely lined by books.

"'Oh, I wouldn't do that, sir,' said Sherman. 'It's rather damp, and there's a draught from the ventilator. You'll find it very chilling. I should sit by the fire.'

"He couldn't disguise the fact that he was an educated man.

"'All right,' I said. After all, I could move as soon as he had gone. I pulled the armchair up to the fire, and added, 'I hope there's plenty of oil in the lamps. I may be sitting up late.' In fact I had made up my mind not to go to bed at all. As soon as I was alone, and the door had shut (sound died very quickly in that old house. I never heard Sherman move away down the passage), I started to do some thinking. And there was a lot to think about.

"They had killed the old lady, that I knew. But why in the name of Providence had they done it? She was overpaying them – and those sort of jobs were few and far between. They were not a stupid pair. Far from it. Yet they had done a foolish thing. They must have known the value of everything in the house. The heavy, unfashionable furniture, riddled with woodworm. The carpets which looked regal in the dim light, but fell to pieces the moment you tried to prise them off the floor. A few clothes and a very few jewels. The whole lot would go to probate for less than a thousand pounds. And on the debit side of the account a sheaf of bad debts and an overdraft at the bank. Net result, nothing. Murder for nothing? Impossible. Then murder for what?

"My eye fell on the books and this started a new train of thought. The Wapentake library had been a good one—"

"I thought I remembered the name," said Bohun. "'Mercy'

41

Martensen was a well-known eighteenth-century collector, wasn't he? A friend of Horace Walpole. He was a nob on Elizabethan poetry and Court Chronicles. I'm sorry. Please go on."

"Not at all," said Mr. Tucker. "That's very interesting. I knew the library was valuable, but I hadn't realised it was historic. Everything in it of value had been disposed of in the salerooms over the last, lean, twenty years. But the thought which had occurred to me was this. Suppose that there were books – one really valuable book would do – which we had overlooked. The library had never been offered as a whole, and the books which had been sold had not been selected on any very logical principle. Outstanding ones, like the *Book of Masques*, had gone early on – Christabel had lived on that book for nearly three years. But I felt a doubt whether any instructed person had gone right through the collection."

"But how—?" said Bohun, and stopped. "Oh, I see. You thought that Mr. Sherman might have been knowledgeable enough to spot a winner if he saw one?"

"Yes. And it made sense of their insistence that 'all the contents' should pass to them. Really, it would have been such a – such a safe crime."

"Foolproof," said Bohun. "Can't you see the story in the newspapers? Devoted old couple get left a houseful of worthless junk. The exciting discovery that among the rubbish has come to light some priceless book. The sale at Sotheby's and the final close-up of the old pair fading away into well-earned retirement clasping a large cheque."

"I am not sure," said Mr. Tucker, "that I thought it all out there and then, but I remember getting up, picking up one of the lamps and starting a sort of search. It was hopeless, of course. You could have put the most valuable book in the world right down in front of me and I would have lacked the skill to identify it. But I did think of one thing. I walked over to the recess where I had first intended to sit, held the lamp up and looked about me. No sign of damp. No draught. Not even a ventilator.

"Then why, I asked myself, had Mr. Sherman troubled to lie about it? There was no question of a misunderstanding. He had said, quite clearly, 'Don't sit there. It's damp. There's a draught through the ventilator.' Following my previous train of thought, I argued that if there was a valuable book they would not dare remove it from the library, since that would arouse just those suspicions they were anxious to avoid. But they might move it into some out-of-the-way corner, and this was the dimmest corner in the library. So I got the ladder and climbed up to the top shelf, and there, in the darkest angle, between two large volumes, I certainly found a curious book. Whether it was valuable or not, I couldn't say, even now. Would you care for something? I myself have a glass of warm milk at this hour."

The maid had come into the room, but Bohun had been so engrossed that he had not heard her.

"What – oh, milk will suit me. What sort of book was it?"

"I took it back to the light," said Mr. Tucker, "and examined it. The outer cover was a sort of yellowish wallet – it had once been white, I suppose – of vellum. The inside came right out, and was a series of pages, some old, of parchment, others rather newer, of paper. When I looked more closely I saw that at some time – the work was by no means recent – the original parchment pages had been taken apart and interleaved. I looked first at the writing on the parchment, but I couldn't make a lot of it, except that it was in English. The letters were difficult. There was nothing to choose between 'n' and 'u' and 'v', and the 'e' looked like an 's' and the 's' like a straggly 'f '."

"Extremely interesting," said Bohun. "Was there writing on the interleaving?"

"Yes. A transcription of what was on the parchment, or so I judged. It was old-fashioned writing, such as I've seen in legal deeds, but perfectly legible. It was a play. I've never been a reader, apart from the law" —Mr. Tucker glanced with apologetic pride at his bookcases— "but once I had got into it, do you know, I found it interesting. It was about a family – I can't remember many of the names – but this girl was very beautiful and was being wooed by a boy who lived near her home. The boy had a so-called friend, but he was a bad lot really. He told a nobleman, who was his patron – the friend's patron – about this girl, and the nobleman lured her away. He was actually helped by the girl's mother, Megira. *She* wasn't a very nice character, either. The boy went after the girl to try and rescue her. The queen of the country, who was on a progress, was staying near the nobleman's house. The boy appealed to her, but the nobleman and Megira told the queen a lot of lies, and she refused even to give him audience. The boy had a friend, a sort of clown, called Euthio, who was always trying to comfort him. Rather a superior sort of man for a clown. I suppose this is all terribly difficult for you to follow."

"Far from it," said Bohun. "Tell me, are you familiar with the works of Scott?"

Mr. Tucker's face lighted up. "Of course, of course," he said. "I think I have them all. His book on Contingent Remainders is the one I have found most useful."

"Not that Scott," said Bohun. "Another one."

"Oh," said Mr. Tucker. "Yes. You mean the novelist. I'm afraid that I've never found much time for that sort of reading."

"Then that," said Bohun, "makes it even more interesting. Can you recall anything that was said in the play? What form was it in? Some sort of verse?"

"Well, it didn't rhyme. Most of it was in – what would you call it? – blank verse. That's right. One line sticks in my memory. When Euthio was talking to the boy, trying to comfort him, you see. He said: 'What Time has swallowed comes not forth again.' I thought that rather neat. In fact, it was all a good readable yarn and a lot of it was very nicely expressed. I got quite engrossed.

"I never heard the door open. And when I suddenly saw that woman's face behind me, I thought for a second it was Megira! She had some heavy thing in her hand and she slashed at my head with it. It was the woodworm that saved me. I had noticed that the chair was rickety, and as I twisted round sharply one of the chair-legs snapped right off, so I was already falling sideways when the thing hit my head, and instead of breaking my skull, it only dazed me. I had the sense to lie still. I could see Mrs. Sherman's face from where I lay. There was no room for doubt. She was quite mad. She must have been going that way for some time and the shock of what I had told her at dinner had toppled her over.

"I don't think she had much idea of what she was doing. She stood for a few minutes peering round the bookshelves, then she picked up the lighted lamp and tossed it on to the floor. It went plop and there was a woof of flame and the paraffin ran all over the carpet with the fire chasing after it. I scrambled up on to my knees. If she saw me, she took no notice. She picked up the other two lamps, and tossed them down too. Then she went out and I heard her shut and lock the door. It was awkward for a moment because the windows up my end of the room were all the thin sort which you open at the top with a rope. Then I remembered there was another door in the corner beside the fireplace. I ran through and found myself in an annexe. It had larger windows, of plain glass, and I stood on the sill, kicked a hole and climbed out. I rolled down the grass bank into a flower bed, and then fainted off properly."

"Good gracious me, yes," said Bohun. "Of course, I remember now. The house was burned to a shell. And the Shermans with it."

"He was in bed. They doubt if he ever woke up. She was in the dining room, what was left of her, when they got the fire out. At some stage in the proceedings I must have been found by the firemen, or the police, and packed off to hospital. Anyway, I had plenty of time to think things out, and I said that I had been in my bedroom, but not undressed, when the fire caught me. It was too late for the stairs, so I dropped from my bedroom window. Which happened to be just above where they found me. Nobody questioned my story. The fire had obviously started in the library and, as Mrs. Sherman was the only one downstairs, it was assumed that she had started it, by accident, when putting the lamps out. The insurance company paid up, and the cousins got what was left after the mortgages had been paid off."

"But," said Bohun, in a rather desperate voice, "didn't you—did you—did anyone—I mean, was there nothing left of the library?"

"Not a scrap," said Mr. Tucker cheerfully. "The brigade said it was one of the fiercest fires they had seen. An absolute furnace. The old woodwork burned like tinder."

"'Not a wrack'," said Bohun. "'Leave not a wrack behind.' 'Such stuff as dreams are made of.'"

He said all this to himself, as he walked slowly along the north side of the Common. He was trying to believe something.

To believe that it was possible that the one, complete, lost play of William Shakespeare, the one that all scholars know about but none had been able to find, the one that fear of the queen had confined to a single version in the poet's own hand, that even after the queen's death could not be put on any stage while the Leicester faction had power to stop it, the original of *Kenilworth* and a dozen stories and legends beside, the tragedy of Amy Robsart; lost to sight after Shakespeare's death, lighted on and transcribed by that eccentric but knowledgeable bibliophile, 'Mercy' Martensen, standing unremarked on the Wapentake library shelves through five generations of port-drinking, pheasant-shooting Martensens; that this unimaginable treasure, as rich as *Antony*, more lurid than *Hamlet*, part of the birthright of the civilised world, had been revealed at the last to Mr. Tucker, who had read it carefully, through one long autumn evening, and had found it a good yarn, and nicely expressed.

Bohun looked back at the front of Mr. Tucker's house, winking in the sun; at the neat lawn and at the plaster dwarf beside the plaster mushroom.

"What Time has swallowed comes not forth again."

He shook his head angrily and jumped on the bus that would take him back to Lincoln's Inn.

The System

"Businessmen don't do it," said Bohun. "Doctors don't. Accountants don't. Even Government Departments have had to give it up. Why are solicitors the only people who hang on to their papers for ever and ever?"

"It can be extremely helpful," said old Mr. Craine.

"Does being able to settle occasional minor points justify the expense of three strong-rooms in Bell Yard, a Nissen hut in Crawley, a warehouse in Slough, and an old wine cellar at Ware? To say nothing of the services of a highly paid muniments' clerk."

"Come, come. You're not suggesting we get rid of Sergeant Cockerill?"

"Certainly not. But he'll soon be wanting to retire. If only we could harden our hearts and send every blessed scrap of paper which is more than ten years old to the incinerator—"

"*Ten* years?"

"Well, twelve at a pinch. We've got stuff going right back to Abel Horniman's youth."

Abel Horniman, a legendary figure in Lincoln's Inn, had founded the firm of Horniman, Brewer and Coates in the nineteen-eighties.

"It was all very well for him," Bohun went on. "In his day you could get a legal assistant for a hundred pounds a year and articled clerks worked for nothing."

These were Bohun's feelings on the matter. And that was how he continued to feel – until the day that Herbert Bellinger had made an appointment to see him.

Herbert was preceded by a letter in the morning post, handwritten in greenish-purple ink, on thick paper. The signature at the end was indecipherable. Bohun went in search of his senior partner. Mr. Craine looked at the signature, tut-tutted, turned back to the address, and said, "That's Miss Louise Bellinger."

"Herbert's Aunt Louie?"

"That's right. Herbert's her brother Arthur's only son. Arthur and his wife – what *was* her name? Millicent, that's right – they were both killed in a motor accident in the late Thirties. She took the boy over. A nice old lady, but practically ga-ga."

"But Aunt Louie's *your* client. I've only met her once."

"We had a difference of opinion. It was about her cats. I agreed with her that Siamese are exceptionally intelligent animals, and I had no real objection to her leaving all her money to them, but when she wanted to make one of them her executor I had to draw the line. That was ten years ago, and I imagined she'd gone to other solicitors. This sounds like an olive branch. What does she want you to do?"

Bohun cast his eye down the long scrawl.

"Nothing much," he said. "It's mostly gossip. She says Herbert's in town today and can I see him? I wonder what he's turned out like? I haven't seen him since he was in short trousers. His aunt brought him up here on his way to school. He sat in the corner and cried."

"A lot of boys cry when they go back to school."

"It was nothing to do with going to school. He was crying because he had a stomach ache. He was sick in the passage."

"I expect he'll have improved," said Mr. Craine soothingly. "What does he want us to do?"

"He wants me to sign his passport application."

Bohun's visitor turned out to be an agreeable man in his middle thirties, with a nondescript face, an engaging smile and a pair of very wide-awake, dark brown eyes. He said, "I can still remember that exact spot in the passage where I was sick. *And* the man who appeared with a pail and mop."

"That'd be Sergeant Cockerill," said Bohun. "He's still with us."

"You don't change much, do you?"

"A firm of family solicitors," said Bohun, "is one of the few unchanging things in a changing world. How is your Aunt Louie these days?"

"It'd be an exaggeration to say she's improving. I'm afraid the time is coming when you'll have to do – whatever it is you do when someone can't cope."

"If she's really becoming incapable of managing her own affairs," said Bohun, "we might have to apply to the Court of Protection, and appoint a receiver."

After his visitor had gone, he reported all this to Mr. Craine who rubbed his hands together, and said, "Splendid, splendid. It looks as though we should get the family business back. I hate losing clients. If you're going to take them on, Henry, you'd better do some background reading."

Accordingly Bohun descended, two evenings later, to the cellarage below the office which was the kingdom of Sergeant Cockerill, the muniments' clerk. The sergeant was small and brown, and looked more like an old mole than an old soldier. His black button eyes brightened at Bohun's request.

"You want *everything* I've got on the Bellinger family?"

"Is there much of it?"

"I've got two boxes here, and several more down at Crawley."

"I'd forgotten they were such active clients."

"They're quieter now. Nothing in the last years but a house purchase for young Dr. Vaisey and a will for the Marlins."

"What have the Vaiseys and Marlins got to do with the Bellingers?"

"They're Henry Bellinger's grandchildren."

"Henry?"

"The one who went wrong on the Stock Exchange."

Bohun thought back, and placed Henry Bellinger with an effort. The dying echoes of that particular scandal had still been rumbling round the office when he first joined the firm.

"Then there was Alfred. He was the younger son."

"He was the one who married the Bishop of Putney's daughter. It broke up, didn't it?"

"That's right," said Cockerill. "And the Bishop preached a sermon about him, names and all, and we had that big slander action."

"I think I'll start with the immediate family. Let me have anything you've got about Aunt Louie, and Cousin Herbert." "I'm not sure we've got anything much on Herbert." Bohun thought about his visitor of that morning, businesslike and self-possessed. Not the sort of person who would trouble his lawyers much.

"We've got a few files about his father and mother." Cockerill thumbed through his card index. "Arthur and Millicent Bellinger. You remember that accident? A shocking tragedy."

After dinner in his flat that evening Bohun settled down to enjoy himself. He had suffered, for thirty years, from parainsomnia, and very rarely got more than ninety minutes sleep in a night. The pile of orange and green files and folders, heaped on the table, overflowing on to a sofa and the floor, promised hours of stimulating reading . . .

Bohun was interested to note how history repeated itself. On 14th October, 1929, Herbert's parents, Arthur and Millicent Bellinger, had presented themselves before Abel Horniman so that he might vouch their application for a passport. But whereas Bohun had scribbled a two-line note, Abel had left a forty-line memorandum, covering not only the application, but other topics, too. "Arthur was worried about the state of the American stock market. I told him not to upset himself. It would certainly recover."

Bohun was still smiling over this remarkable prediction when he picked up the copies which Abel had made of the applications he had been asked to sign.

When he had read them through twice, he looked at his watch. It was one o'clock in the morning, but there was a government line which was manned night and day. Bohun called the number and spoke at some length. Then he rang off and returned to the files. The minutes ticked past.

At three o'clock, a car slid up to Bohun's door and his bell rang. He went down.

His caller introduced himself, without prefix, as Shipman. He was a slightly built man, with a brown face and wiry grey hair, who might have been any age from forty to sixty. His voice, which was equally unrevealing, could have come from any class or region. He could even have been a foreigner who spoke exceptionally good English.

"I have come round to check up on one or two points," he said. "Have you got the papers here – the ones you mentioned?"

Bohun produced the careful transcripts of the passport application forms which Abel Horniman had pinned into the file over forty years ago.

"You see," he said. "Arthur Bellinger. Eyes, light blue. His wife, Millicent, the same. It would be excessively long odds for two parents with china-blue eyes to produce a son with dark brown eyes. Not impossible. There might be a regressive strain. You'd have to know about the grandparents to be certain. But I thought it needed checking. *Was* the man who turned up in my office Herbert Bellinger?"

"No," said Shipman. "He wasn't."

"You've checked the application?"

"Yes," said Shipman. "We've checked it."

He opened his wallet and pulled out a photograph. It was the one Bohun had signed. Then he extracted another photograph, an enlarged snapshot of a man leaving an office building. They were clearly the same.

"Who is he?" asked Bohun.

Shipman appeared to consider the point. Then, instead of answering Bohun directly, he said, "How did you know what number to ring up just now?"

"I did a bit of work last year for Colonel Heseltine. Nothing complicated. Just a bit of cross-checking."

Shipman said, "Ah. I wondered. Well, this chap is William Austin. Born in Roysfield, started as a barrister with the Director of Public Prosecutions. Did very well. Then he joined us. We've been worried about him for some time. If he'd tried to get out of England on his own passport, he'd have been stopped. That's why he had to get a new one. As Herbert Bellinger, he'd a chance of getting through. It isn't a very remarkable face.

"It was a risky way of doing it," said Bohun. "I thought any crook with money could buy a new passport."

Shipman smiled faintly. "Suppose you wanted one. How would you set about it?"

"Me? I haven't the faintest idea. But then I'm not a crook."

"Nor is Austin. And if he tried to contact a professional criminal, he really would have been in trouble."

"He must have known Herbert well. Some of his background patter was terribly convincing. And, come to think of it, he must have known that Herbert hadn't already got a passport."

"Not necessarily. This application was made under expedited procedure. If you put up a convincing story – a dying relative whose bedside you're hurrying to – your application goes to the top of the queue and you can get your passport in forty-eight hours. In a case like that there isn't time to check against all existing applications. So it wouldn't necessarily be noticed that there were two Herbert Bellingers. Neither name's all that uncommon—"

Bohun was staring at his visitor in consternation. "Do you mean to say that he actually *got* his passport and is already out of the country?"

"He got his passport all right. He picked it up this evening – yesterday evening, I should say. But it hasn't been presented at any exit point."

"Would it be serious if he did get out?"

"It wouldn't be serious," said Shipman. "It'd be a disaster. He was high enough in D.I.6 to know the names and cover stories of every single one of our agents in Eastern Europe."

Bohun thought again of the man with the nondescript face, the engaging smile and the wide-awake, brown eyes. He said, "You never can tell, can you?"

"When you counter-signed his application form," said Shipman, "I've no doubt you were strictly correct in saying that you had known the applicant for twenty-five years. But you realise that it isn't intended to cover a case where you haven't seen him in the interval."

"I do realise it," said Bohun unhappily. "And it's no excuse to say that I think most people would have been fooled. I'll go down today and see Miss Bellinger. She might tell me something useful, though I doubt it. She'd be easy meat for a plausible man like Austin. And I could have a word with Herbert – if he's available. If there's anything else I can do to help locate Austin—"

Shipman smiled again, a faint glimmer of professional amusement. He said, "By acting so quickly, Mr. Bohun, you've gone a long way to atone for your original carelessness. Certainly have a word with both the Bellingers. But as for locating Austin, I doubt if that will be necessary. We shall pick him up now as soon as he tries to use his false passport. And even if we don't, we shall have the whole of D.I.6, the Special Branch *and* the regular police mobilised to trace him—"

It was at that point that the telephone rang. Bohun answered it, and said, "They seem to know you're here."

Shipman picked up the receiver without haste, and listened without visible change of expression. At the end he said, "Very well. I'll come back as quickly as I can."

He said nothing more. Bohun was longing to know what development had sent him scurrying back, but realised that his curiosity was unlikely to be satisfied.

In fact, his visitor was actually getting into his car before he decided to speak. He said, "Austin presented that passport at Heathrow, half an hour ago. When he spotted that there was going to be trouble, he ran for it. They haven't picked him up yet."

Bohun stood in the street and watched the tail-lights of the car disappear. Then he slowly climbed the stairs back to his flat. A thin light was beginning to come back into the sky. It was clear to him that he wasn't going to get his ration of sleep that night. He put on the kettle, made himself a cup of coffee, and finished his reading of the Bellinger family files.

At ten o'clock that morning he called on Miss Louise Bellinger at her house in Hertfordshire. She received him in a decaying morning room, turned a resentful Siamese cat off the sofa, and invited him to sit down. Bohun had wondered how he was going to explain the real motives for his visit, but she saved him the trouble.

"Do you think," she said, "that I'm going mad?"

"Of course not."

"Well, I think I am. Have a look at that. It came this morning."

It was a letter scribbled on two sides of a sheet of thin foreign notepaper. Bohun turned to the end, and read, "Yours affectionately, Herbert." He then turned back to the beginning and saw that the address was Salzkammergut, in the Austrian Dolomites, and that it was dated four days before. Light dawned.

"That's all right," he said.

"It's *not* all right," said Miss Bellinger. "That's the whole point. It's all wrong. I'm beginning to have illusions. Terribly graphic illusions. Four days ago – on the very day this was written – a young man came into this room. I couldn't recall his name, but I knew him by sight. He was a friend of Herbert's. Herbert had sent him. He wanted me to write a letter to a Mr. Bohun – he's that old donkey Craine's junior partner—"

"That's me," said Bohun.

The old lady peered at him in mild surprise, and said, "Oh, that's who you are, is it? You don't look much like a lawyer."

"Did this man say *why* Herbert couldn't have come along himself?"

"He was busy doing something. I've really forgotten what it was. Does it matter ?"

"Not a bit," said Bohun. "Please go on."

"Well, that's all. He said it was urgent, so I sat down and wrote the letter. He posted it for me."

"I see," said Bohun.

"Well, I *don't*. If Herbert was already abroad, why should he need a passport?"

"I'm afraid this man was lying to you."

"What a very curious thing to do. Of course, people nowadays haven't got the same regard for truth. Stop it, you brute!" This was to the resentful cat which had emerged from ambush under Miss Bellinger's chair and buried its claws in her ankle.

She kicked at it deftly, and it disappeared, in spitting fury, under the sofa.

"There's one thing I would like to know," said Bohun. "You said you recognised this young man. Can you remember where you'd seen him before?"

"At a wedding."

"Whose?"

The old lady shook her head. "You can't expect me to remember things like that," she said. "It was a family wedding. A very pretty one. He sat on the other side of the church to us, and came and talked to us afterwards. Herbert and he found they'd been at school together – or it may have been at college. I can't remember anything else."

As soon as he got back to the office, Bohun sent for Sergeant Cockerill. He said, "I want *all* the files we've got on the Bellinger family. Not just Herbert and Aunt Louie, the lot."

"Right back to Sir Rawnsley Bellinger?"

"Back to Adam, if we go back that far."

"I don't remember an Adam Bellinger."

"Skip it," said Bohun. "I was speaking metaphorically. I meant, go back as far as our records go."

"It'll be quite a big job. I'll have to go down to Slough and Crawley and may be to Ware as well. Is it an urgent job?"

"It's not just urgent. It's a job of national importance. Hire a car. Make a round trip. The firm will pay."

By that evening the fruits of the sergeant's round trip were completely filling one end of Bohun's sitting room. Eight black japanned tin boxes, two tea chests, a pile of deed wallets, a stack of letter files, and an old, brown leather suitcase, which turned out to contain the full-dress levée uniform, complete with sword, which Sir Rawnsley Bellinger had deposited with Abel Horniman in 1888.

Bohun started with the tin box labelled, *Sir Rawnsley Bellinger, Marriage Settlement* and set out to reconstruct the family.

Sir Rawnsley had sired three boys and a girl. Henry, the eldest, born in 1890 had, at the early age of twenty-one, married a French girl, Celestine Legrange. Bohun pictured her as a fluffy little thing whose extravagance had driven Henry to his unfortunate financial crash. Their daughter, Lettice, married George Vaisey in 1934. *That* wedding could be ruled out. Herbert would have been one year old at the time.

There were two children, Christopher Vaisey, a doctor, as yet unmarried, and Agnes, who married Hugo Marlin in 1957. Distinctly more possible. Herbert would be twenty-four, just down from Oxford. And the marriage was long enough ago for Aunt Louie to have forgotten all the details. File that one for reference.

Ruling out Aunt Louie, and her brother, Arthur, who had married Millicent and produced Herbert, that left only Sir Rawnsley's youngest child, Alfred. Married in 1932, to Margaret Parker, daughter of the Bishop of Putney. Marriage dissolved in 1937. No children. Second marriage in 1939 to a Miss Broach. A gap, represented no doubt, by the war, then six children in rapid succession; but the eldest only born in 1947 and all unmarried as yet. So it must have been the Agnes Vaisey – Hugo Marlin wedding. And if Austin had been sitting 'on the other side of the church', he must have been a friend of the Marlins *before* he met Herbert at school or university.

Bohun proceeded to concentrate on the Marlin side of the family.

Fortunately, they had been clients for almost as long as the Bellingers. A busy set – with settlements, wills and deeds of family arrangement. Hugo was an insurance broker, who had taken over his father-in-law George Vaisey's business and expanded into half a dozen profitable lines.

Bohun took five large pieces of paper. In the centre of each he inscribed a name – George Vaisey, Lettice Bellinger, Christopher Vaisey, Hugo Marlin and Agnes Vaisey. He then proceeded to write round them, in concentric circles, the names of all the people who had been connected with them, in private life or in business: the trustees and beneficiaries of their settlements; the people who had witnessed their own and their family's wills; their partners, the secretaries and directors of the half dozen companies with whom they had been concerned, and the names of the other companies of which those directors had, in turn, themselves been directors. Hugo seemed to have been an uncommonly quarrelsome man, and one circle comprised the people against whom he had litigated, and the names of the witnesses on both sides.

Lettice Bellinger had been a compulsive letter writer, both before and after her marriage to George Vaisey, and her correspondence produced a whole catalogue of names which, in turn, produced further names, and those names suggested different avenues of research.

Six o'clock was sounding faintly from the clocks in the Strand when Bohun straightened his aching back, and regarded his first night's work with satisfaction.

There were nearly a thousand names on the sheets of paper, *but they were by no means a thousand different names.* It was extraordinary how the same people recurred in quite different contexts. It was like seeing your favourite character actor, thought Bohun, turning up in half a dozen different parts. For instance, a man who had been a secretary in one of George Vaisey's early companies, and had witnessed his will (the first of three that he made), had married a distant Marlin cousin, subsequently divorced her, and was now a director in one of the Marlin company's main competitors, and had featured in the big patent dispute three years before.

William Austin's name had appeared in several different capacities, and each time Bohun had underscored it heavily in red. His mother had been a friend of the Miss Broach who had been Alfred Bellinger's second wife. He had been a contemporary of Herbert's, both at school and university, and had spent one complete holiday with him, a fact which Aunt Louie had evidently forgotten.

His acquaintanceship with Hugo Marlin had arisen because they used the same church and had been involved in the troubles of its vicar, who had been forced to resign over a matter concerning choirboys. Marlin had used his influence to get Austin started at the Bar, but then seemed to have drifted out of his life. Quite a few other people had drifted into it, however, leaving their footprints in the sands of time and in the records of Horniman, Brewer and Craine.

Bohun shaved and breakfasted, and reached the office in time to get hold of the various assistants he wanted. One went to Somerset House, another to the Companies Registry, and young Rowley was dispatched to a newspaper-cutting service which he had used before and which kept, as he knew, a back-numbers section.

Bohun tackled one or two routine jobs that morning, but was unable to concentrate on them. More than half his mind was pursuing the winding tracks of William Austin through the mazes of a solicitor's records. Soon after lunch he abandoned the effort and went back to his flat, where he found Sergeant Cockerill unloading a further cargo of files.

"You'll know something about this family before you've finished," he said approvingly. "That lot's Sir Rawnsley's brother's family, the Chatterton-Taylors. I'd forgotten we had them. They married into the Carew family, but we don't act for them."

At five o'clock Rowley arrived with a bundle of press-cuttings and stared in amazement at the scene in Bohun's room.

"What on earth are you doing?" he said. "Programming a computer?"

"In a way," said Bohun.

"What do all those colours mean? Who's the one you've underlined in red?"

"That's a man called William Austin."

"Never heard of him."

"You will," said Bohun. "You will."

Rowley looked at him curiously. He had a great respect for Bohun. "You're not pulling my leg, are you?"

"Certainly not. This is one of the most serious pieces of research I have ever undertaken."

"Who are the blues and greens and purples and yellows?"

"It's a colour code. They are the people who feature most often in Austin's life. The darker the colour, the closer the association."

Rowley had been leaning forward to read the names in Bohun's microscopic handwriting. Now he straightened up and pulled a sheaf of cuttings from his pocket. "You'll find quite a few of them here," he said. "Look, there's a purple for a start, and a green, and a brown."

Bohun said, "What's that one you've got there?"

"It's a list of the guests at the Vaisey-Marlin wedding. It wasn't actually published, but this place keeps them. They sometimes come in useful."

"Useful?"

"Well, you never know. The best man might rape one of the bridesmaids. I say, can I help? It looks rather fun."

"If you promise to keep your mouth shut," said Bohun.

An hour later, Rowley, looking down a long list of legatees in a will said, "It's rather like Happy Families, isn't it? Have you got Master Bones, the Butcher's son? No, but you can oblige me with Mrs. Block, the Barber's wife? Talking about Block, here's Colonel Block turned up again. What's he?"

"Outer fringe," said Bohun. "Pale green."

It was two o'clock in the morning when he closed the final file. Rowley had given up an hour before and was fast asleep on the sofa. Bohun gazed at the completed pattern: the assets and liabilities, the lives and loves, the hopes and fears of a group of people, seen through the peep-hole of a solicitor's practice. The colours around the red had sorted themselves out in a remarkable way. The predominance of the purple, the blue and the scarlet was apparent to the naked eye. He reached for the telephone.

Shipman answered it. He said, "No, we haven't traced him yet. We've checked all the normal places. Hotels, boarding houses, bed-and-breakfast places, brothels, Turkish baths, and main-line stations. He may have spent two nights under a hedge, but he can't keep that up. He'll show up soon."

"You've checked on his family?"

"Of course."

"And his friends?"

Shipman said, the lack of two nights' sleep lending a ragged edge to his voice, "Unfortunately we don't happen to possess a directory of his friends. If we did, of course we could check them."

"That's what I rather thought," said Bohun. "Austin's a sensible chap. He's been a sort of policeman himself. He knows the routine. The place he'd make for would be the house of a *friend*. But not one with too obvious a connection. Someone who'd helped him out in the past, and would do so again, if he spun them a convincing yarn."

"Have you got any ideas?"

"I can give you three names and addresses. There's a man called Lewis. Averill Lewis. A barrister, not now practising. He paid Austin's debts for him at Oxford, and helped him at the Bar. He's got a country cottage. I'll give you the address. Next candidate, the Reverend Arthur Champerdowne – spelt with an 'e'. Used to have a North London living, now incumbent of a small Kentish parish. There could be an element of blackmail there. Third, Mrs. Chatterton-Taylor. She's shown a motherly interest in Austin on a number of occasions. Extremely motherly. If you hang on, I'll give you her address, too."

"Well, thank you," said Shipman.

Shipman thanked Bohun again, more officially, when Austin was discovered hiding in a back room of the Reverend Champerdowne's rambling vicarage.

A long time afterwards, when the trial was over, and the sensation had faded out of the paper, Bohun told his senior partner all about it.

Old Mr. Graine was not in the least surprised. "The Special Branch, the Secret Service, the Police," he said. "No doubt they're all right in their own way. But they haven't got our facilities."

Cousin Once Removed

When Kenneth Alworthy said to his cousin Arthur, "I've fixed to take a little fishing holiday in early June. I'm going to a farm in Cumberland. It's got two miles of fishable water and I'm told it's as lonely as the Sahara Desert," Arthur (himself a fisherman) felt that peculiar thrill which comes when, after the casting of successive flies, each gaudy, each attractive, each subtly different, the big trout is seen to rise ponderously from the peaty recesses under the river bank and cock his eye at the lure.

Arthur had wrought hard and long for this moment.

Almost a year ago he had mentioned Howorth's Farm to his cousin. He had done it casually – so casually that Kenneth had already forgotten who had told him about it. Twice thereafter he had mentioned it to friends who, he guessed, would pass it on to Kenneth. Then, in March, at the time when the first daffodils look out and far-sighted people plan their holidays, he had sent a copy of a Cumberland newspaper to his cousin. In it he had marked for him an account of the newly discovered rock fissure below Rawnmere, for Kenneth was an amateur of speleology.

But it was not only the marked paragraph that he had counted on Kenneth seeing. Immediately below it was the five-line advertisement which the owner of Howorth's Farm put into the local press each spring.

After that Arthur left it alone.

If a trout will not rise there is no profit in thrashing the water.

If you were asked, why was it so important to one cousin that the other cousin go apparently of his own free will, to a particular farm in

61

Cumberland, then you would have to cast widely for the answer.

First you would have to examine the will of their common grandfather, Albert Alworthy, who had made his money out of quarrying, and tied it up tightly.

His solicitor, Mr. Rumbold (the father of the present senior partner), had drawn the will, and his client's instructions had been clear. "Tie it up as tight as the law allows," said the old man. "To my children, and then to their children, and the survivor can have the lot. I dug it out of the earth by the sweat of my brow. Let them sweat for it."

Fifty years later Mr. Rumbold, Junior, had attempted to explain these provisions to Arthur.

"Two wars thinned you out a lot," he said. "Your father and your cousin Kenneth's father – that was your Uncle Bob – were the only two of old Albert's children who had any children themselves. And you and your cousin are the only two grandchildren left."

"And so it goes to Kenneth and me?"

"To the survivor of Kenneth and you."

"How much—about?"

The solicitor named a sum, and Arthur Alworthy pursed his lips.

He wanted money. He wanted it badly, and he wanted it fairly quickly. Not next week, or even next month, but if he didn't get it in a year he was done for. Certain bills were maturing steadily. He might borrow to meet them, but borrowing more money in order to meet existing debts is an improvident form of economy, even for a man with expectations. And even borrowing could not keep him afloat for more than a year at most.

A second reason for the selection of Howorth's Farm lay in a personal tragedy which had befallen Arthur some years before, when walking in the neighbourhood. He had lost his dog, an attractive but inquisitive cocker spaniel, down a pot-hole in the moor. It was a deep, ugly-looking hole, partly masked by undergrowth and surrounded by a rusty and unstable wire fence. Had it existed in a less lonely spot its dangers would have led to proper precautions being taken. As it was, it was fully three miles from Howorth's Farm, and the farm was five miles from the nearest village. A few of the shepherds knew of the pot-hole's existence and it was to one of them that Arthur had hurried, hoping there might be some way of saving the animal.

The shepherd had shaken his head with the quiet firmness of a man who tells an unpleasant truth.

"Nothing come alive out of that pot," he said. "Poor little beggar, but you can reckon he'll be dead by now. It's not a dry pot, you see, Mister. There's a scour of water at the bottom." Twenty years ago, continued the shepherd, a party of experts had gone down to explore. They had found a sheep, which had fallen in a month before. At least, they thought it was a sheep. The icy current and the jagged rocks had done their dissecting work very thoroughly and the evidence was by then inconclusive.

"Another month," said the shepherd, "and there wouldn't have been nothing left at all."

"They ought to put a proper fence around it," Arthur had said, angrily.

"So they ought," the shepherd had agreed, but he had said it without much conviction because, rusty and rickety as it was, the fence was now strong enough to stop a sheep, and that was all he really cared about.

The day after Kenneth packed up his fly rods and left for the north, Arthur went on a walking tour. He went a certain distance by train, and after that he used youth hostels on some nights, and on others nothing at all, for he was an experienced camper, and could make shift for days by himself with a sleeping bag and a small primus stove. Four days later he passed the night in a tangle of thickets just above Howorth's Farm. He had walked twenty miles the day before without putting his foot on a man-made road. He had provisions for seven days with him, *War and Peace* in the three-volume edition, and a strong pair of field glasses. Luckily the weather remained fine.

On the fourth day he saw Kenneth, a walking-stick in his hand instead of a fishing rod, coming up the hill by the path which ran past his encampment.

Hastily brushing himself down he slid out of the undergrowth, and made a detour, striking the path higher up.

Thus the cousins met, face to face, on a turn in the track, out of sight of the farm.

When greetings had been exchanged, Arthur said, "I'm based on a hostel over at Langdale. I thought I'd take a walk in this direction and watch you catch some fish."

"Not today," said Kenneth. "The dry weather has sucked the life out of the stream. The old boy down at the farm swears it's going to rain tonight, and that I'll get some sport tomorrow. Today I'm giving it a rest. Have you any ideas on what it would be fun to do? I don't know the countryside myself."

Arthur pretended to consider.

"It's the best part of three miles," he said, "but let's go and look at that pot-hole I found five years ago."

His cousin was agreeable.

It took them an hour, and Kenneth's life depended solely upon whether they happened to meet anyone. A single shepherd, seeing them from a distance, would have made it necessary for Arthur to choose another time.

They met no one, and no one saw them.

Presently they were gazing down into the hole.

"You can almost hear the water running," said Arthur. "Look out, man – don't lean too far—!"

A month later Arthur sat again in the room of Mr. Rumbold, the solicitor.

"Tragic," said the lawyer. "I don't suppose we shall ever know the truth. He must have gone out for a walk and fallen down one of those holes. There are a lot of them in that district, I understand."

"Dozens," said Arthur, "and it would take a month to explore a single one of them thoroughly."

"You were on holiday, yourself, when it happened?"

"I was on a walking tour. I may have been less than forty miles from the accident when it happened," said Arthur. He never lied unnecessarily.

"A tragic coincidence," said the lawyer.

Towards the end of the interview Arthur broached what was in his mind.

"I suppose," he said, "in the circumstances – I know the formalities will take a little time – but might I be able to have a little money?"

"Well, I'm not sure," said the lawyer.

"But—" Arthur took a firm hold of himself. "You said yourself," he went on, "that it all went to the survivor."

"Can you prove that you are the survivor?"

There was a long pause.

"I suppose not. Not *prove* it. Everyone assumes – I mean, he left all his things at the farm. No one's heard a word from him since."

"The law," said Mr. Rumbold, "is very slow to assume that a man is dead. If, in all the circumstances, it appears probable that a man has died, you will, after a suitable time has elapsed, be permitted to deal with his estate—"

"A suitable time?" said Arthur hollowly.

"Seven years is the usual period."

"Seven years – but it's crazy! Mr. Rumbold, surely, in a case like this, where it's obvious that an accident—"

"*If* Kenneth is dead," said Mr. Rumbold, "and, as I say, the law will presume no such thing from his mere absence, but *if* he is dead, then I am not at all sure that it *was* an accident."

When Arthur had recovered his voice he said, "What do you mean?"

"I tell you this in confidence," said Mr. Rumbold, "as it was told me. But your cousin has been suffering, since the war, from a deteriorating condition of the spine. One specialist had gone so far as to say that he was unlikely to live out the year. I'm afraid he may have made his mind up, perhaps on the spur of the moment, to end himself. So you see—"

Arthur saw. He saw only too clearly.

Modus Operandi

Chief Inspector Hazlerigg, who has recently been promoted to superintendent, came from Norfolk to London at the age of seventeen and started his career pounding a beat in Whitechapel. He has risen by regulation steps at reasonably long intervals. His chief asset is that he looks so honest that no one ever attempts to bribe him. He possesses a rigid sense of right and wrong, which he inherited from his mother, who was a Quaker, and a shrewd ability to see round corners, which came from his father, who was a poacher.

He is very rarely angry about crime. This was one of the rare occasions. But then, in this case he had every reason to be.

Hazlerigg reserved his most intolerant criticisms for what he called 'pinch of dust' detectives.

I think the expression originated in his mind when I told him of a story I had read in a magazine about a detective whose only clue to the identity of a felon was a sample of dust from the turn-ups of his trousers – the felon's trousers, I mean. Microscopic analysis revealed that this dust was composed in equal parts of a green chalk, of grains of sand of a type found only at Bognor Regis, and of particles of powdered granite belonging to a geological stratum which, surprisingly enough, approaches the earth's surface at Bickley. It was then child's play to deduce, look for, and arrest a billiard marker of Bickley who took his summer holidays at Bognor.

"Why?" said Hazlerigg. "Why not an enthusiastic snooker-player from Bognor with relatives at Bickley?"

"Or," suggested Inspector Pickup, "a man who lived at Orpington but worked in a shop at Bickley and had in his back garden a sandpit that his predecessor had stocked with sand from Bognor."

"Or a man who had bought a pair of trousers secondhand from a chap who had exchanged *his* trousers for—"

"All right, all right," I said. "We yield the point. You mean, I take it, that it's no good using these scientific analyses to catch your man."

"Oh, there's nothing wrong with science," said Hazlerigg, broadmindedly. "Once the prisoner's in custody, let science have its head. So long as it's the sort of science a jury will swallow," he added. "It's taken them fifty years to believe in fingerprints."

"Then if you don't catch them by science—?"

Hazlerigg observed the bait, but appeared to accept the hook.

"That's what you've been leading up to all along, isn't it?" he said. "All right, I'll tell you. There's no terrific secret about it. Take burglars. Apart from the ones which are actually caught on the job – and the British householder perpetually amazes me by his willingness to tackle anything up to twice his own weight in armed house-breakers – out of every hundred who eventually get caught, I should say that fifty, at least, run into trouble trying to dispose of the proceeds.

"And it's a sad reflection on human nature," went on Hazlerigg, "but the next biggest group are those who are given away by informers."

"And the rest?"

"Miscellaneous. Hard work and concentration on the M.O. files."

"I've never really understood that," I said. "I mean, I know the principle of *modus operandi*. You are called to a burglary in Hampstead and you find that the pantry window has been forced with a bricklayer's trowel and that the burglar has helped himself to a cup of tea before leaving by the back door. You then trot back to Scotland Yard, turn up the index, and discover that the only man on your books who habitually uses a bricklayer's trowel *and* gains access by pantry windows *and* helps himself to a cup of tea is Smokey Joe. So you send someone off to pull Joe in, and if Joe can't explain his movements last Friday evening, then ten to one he's for it. That's about it, isn't it?"

"More or less."

"But what I don't understand is, why doesn't Joe take the trouble to change his habits? He's only got to open, say, the library window with a pick head, or even wait till he gets home before he has his cup of tea, and he's safe as houses."

"You might think so," said Hazlerigg. "It doesn't work out that way. First, because a lot of the items in the M.O. index are things that he *can't* change or, at least, would be very unlikely to change. The type of stuff he steals – well, that'll depend on what facilities he has for getting rid of it, doesn't it? If his receiver gives him top prices for fur coats, then fur coats he must have. The demand creates the supply. Again, take the question of whether he works alone or not. Now, that's a matter of temperament. He's born with it—"

"In fundamentals, I agree; but what about the little things?"

"Look here," said Hazlerigg. "If I told you that it was vitally important that you shouldn't hitch up the knees of your trousers before sitting down in a chair – as I've noticed once or twice is a habit of yours – if I told you that your life depended on your not doing it, could you *guarantee* that you wouldn't do it again – say, next week?"

"Well—no. Perhaps not. But I don't think that's a fair analogy."

Hazlerigg grinned and looked at Inspector Pickup, who mouthed a word that sounded like 'Copley', and they both laughed.

That was all I got out of them, at the time. The story was still on the secret file. I heard the rest of it some time later.

During the aftermath of the late war, at a time when all the crime charts were rocketing, Scotland Yard started to become conscious of the activities of a new burglar. All criminals whose work is both distinctive and successful – successful, I mean, from the criminal's point of view – are apt to acquire simple nicknames and this burglar was known to the police of the Metropolis and Home Counties as the Flat Man (because he specialised in flats) or more commonly as the Neat Man, because he never left many traces of his visit, unless you can call the absence of the owner's silver, jewellery, and clothing a trace. He was also called the Neat Man for another reason which will presently appear.

"He works single-handed," said Hazlerigg, when he was presenting an analysis to the Assistant Commissioner (the Neat Man had become as important as that). "And either he is the most marvellous lock-picker alive or else he has the art of selecting the right key for the right door. He never forces a catch. He never goes through a window. So far as we know, he enters like a gentleman, by the front door, which he opens, as I said, with a key or in some other painless manner."

"Catch locks?" said the Assistant Commissioner.

"Oh, no, sir. Everything. Mortice locks and all. Then there's another thing. He seems to know his way about so uncannily. We can usually pick up his footprints. He has an exceptionally small neat foot and often wears dancing pumps. Many of these expensive flats have wall-to-wall carpets, and when we arrive on the scene before it's been too trodden over, we can follow his progress there and back. It's always the same story. He comes in the front door; he goes straight to the room he wants; he takes what he can find – I mean, he never breaks open cupboards or desks, he just lifts whatever comes handy; then he goes straight back again to the hall – and then there was something used to puzzle us. You'd see his footsteps going straight up the hall. Suddenly, for no reason, they'd stop, there'd be a mark where he'd turned, and a pair of prints pointing sideways, towards the wall, if you follow me. Usually with the toe prints clearer than the heels."

"It sounds quite mad to me," said the Assistant Commissioner. "What did you make of it?"

"We made nothing of it at first," said Hazlerigg. "But when we did spot it, well, it was perfectly obvious. He was a tie-twiddler."

"A what?"

"A tie-twiddler or a hair-smoother, or a lapel-brusher – I mean, he was the sort of man who couldn't pass a looking-glass without stopping for a moment to peer at himself.

Probably did it quite unconsciously. Being on the small side – as his footprints indicate – he usually had to stand on tiptoe. Hence the marks."

"So all we've got to do," said the Assistant Commissioner, "is to search London for a small man who admires himself in looking-glasses." He didn't say it unkindly. He appreciated the difficulties.

Inspector Hazlerigg had found himself in charge of the Neat Man investigation in the fortuitous way that things sometimes happened at Scotland Yard. The Neat Man seemed to specialise in stealing good clothes. The best market for stolen suits is Whitechapel. Hazlerigg had a lot of contacts still in Whitechapel. Therefore, the Neat Man was handed to him. Hazlerigg was neither pleased nor grateful. He had a good deal on his plate already. Nevertheless he made the routine investigations in the same thorough way that he did all his work. All the relevant reports were brought to him and he studied them and analysed them and cross-indexed the results and hoped for a break. Then, one night, the job ceased to be routine.

Hazlerigg was living, at that time, in a furnished flat towards the Highgate end of Hornsey Lane. He came home to it at a quarter to midnight after a long day. He felt very tired. When he got in he went to the sideboard for a tankard of beer and found, to his surprise, that the cupboard was empty. There had been some table silver in it as well as the tankards; also a pair of rather nice small Georgian candle-sticks. They were gone, too. With a sudden sinking feeling he made for his bedroom and opened the wardrobe. "Both suits and my dinner jacket," he said, "curse him!" He reached for the telephone.

"It's Mr. Neat all right," said the divisional detective inspector. "It's got all the trade marks. Here's where he stopped to take a look at himself" – he pointed to a barometer that had been hanging on the wall predicting *Wet to Stormy* ever since Hazlerigg had come into the flat. "No marks of forcing on the door, either. Did you turn the lock when you went out, sir?"

Hazlerigg had the grace to blush. "No," he said. "I forgot."

From that moment he really started putting his back into the job.

First thing next morning he summoned Sergeant Brakewell to his room. What Sergeant Brakewell didn't know about locks could hardly be classified as knowledge.

"How do burglars set about picking locks?" Hazlerigg asked. "In particular, the locks on the doors of flats."

"Well, sir," said Sergeant Brakewell, "it's a big subject, roughly speaking—"

At the end of three-quarters of an hour he paused for breath and Hazlerigg said: "As I understand it, catch locks are easy. You push the tongue back with a stiff bit of talc, or gum the works up with liquid paraffin, and use a plain key. Mortice locks are more difficult, but most real experts have such a fine collection of basic keys – what people call skeleton keys – that they can usually find one to fit. And if it won't quite fit they cover it with lampblack, push it in, look at the scratches, file it down a trifle, and Bob's your uncle."

"That's about it," said Sergeant Brakewell.

"Right. Now, here are the records of more than forty housebreakings. We're pretty certain they are the same man. I'll let you have them to study and I'll arrange for you to see the actual lock itself if you think it'll be helpful – and if you want a recent and untouched specimen," he added grimly, "I have the very thing for you at home."

"So I've heard," said Sergeant Brakewell with a discreet grin.

A week later he made his report.

"I think, sir," he concluded, "that there's no reasonable doubt. In every case the door was opened with a copy of the actual key. As I explained, where the lock's new, a copy key will make very much the same marks as the regular one. But where it's an old lock, one that has developed play, a copy, however careful, will leave marks."

He enumerated them, and Hazlerigg listened a little absent-mindedly.

When Sergeant Brakewell had gone, he opened the classified directory and searched under the house agents until he found the firm he wanted. Then he turned to the records of the cases and went through them again, copying down details.

To Inspector Pickup, two days later, he confided the results of his enquiries.

"I think we're on to something," he said, "though I'm blessed if I can quite see how it works. If Brakewell's right about the keys – and I'd back his judgement in that line against anyone in England – then it means that this burglar must at some time or other have had his hand on the original keys. But then you're up against a difficulty. House keys are things people are apt to be a bit careful with. I mean, they don't leave them lying about or entrust them to perfect strangers. I didn't anyway. I don't think my door key was ever out of my possession."

"But the house agent—"

"Exactly," said Hazlerigg. "So I took the trouble to find out who had acted in the renting of all these flats."

"And they were all handled by the same firm?"

"Not quite," said Hazlerigg. "It was three firms. All North London firms, it's true. But not connected with each other, so far as I know. Start and Baxter of Hornsey, Croppers of Highgate, and Shaw, Shaw, Shaw and Shaw of Hampstead. I'm on my way to see Croppers now."

Messrs. Croppers (*If You Want a House of Character Come to Croppers*) have their estate agency on Highgate Hill. It possesses a low entrance, a step down from the pavement, and black beams alternating with cream plaster: all of which are well known to be signs of Character in a House. Even Mr. Cropper, who wore a Victorian frock coat, had a certain old-fashioned grace about him.

Inspector Hazlerigg introduced himself and explained a small part of what was in his mind. Mr. Cropper said: "We are always very friendly with Start and Baxter – a very nice little firm. But as for Shaw and Shaw, well, you know, Inspector, they're hardly in our line. In fact, they're hardly the sort of firm I'd care to—"

"Of course."

"I should describe them," said Mr. Cropper, "as modern. We here at Croppers have certain old-fashioned traditions, certain prejudices as to what is fair dealing . . ."

Half an hour later Hazlerigg was seated in the chromium and art-leather interior of Messrs. Shaw, Shaw, Shaw and Shaw's estate office in Hampstead. The senior partner, after glancing cautiously at the Chief Inspector's card, said: "Yes, I know Croppers very well. We have as little to do with them as we can. This is an up-to-the-minute business and we try to run it on up-to-the-minute lines."

He glanced complacently at the six huge olive-green steel filing cabinets. "I can't think of any possible—er—line of connection between us. I don't even recollect that we've ever taken on one of their employees. Nor, so far as I know, have any of our employees stepped—er—down to join them."

Mr. Baxter, of Start and Baxter, a little sandy-haired man who worked in a three-room office in Hornsey, proved the most helpful and the easiest to deal with; and in return Hazlerigg told him a great deal more of the truth than he had exposed to either of his rivals.

"Let me see," said Mr. Baxter. "We got your flat for you, didn't we? I thought I recognised you—yes—well, now about those other firms. I don't really have a great deal to do with them—now."

Hazlerigg looked up sharply.

"It used to be different – just after the end of the war, when everybody wanted flats and houses, and people were lining up for anything and everything. There used to be a certain amount of splitting commissions, among the established firms, and I worked in with the Shaws and Croppers on one or two deals. The idea, from our point of view, was to keep the mushroom business out of it – and it suited the public too. It meant that they could use two or three different firms to sell their houses without the risk of having to pay two or three commissions."

"But you didn't work together over all these jobs—" Hazlerigg pointed to his list.

"Oh, Lord, no," said Mr. Baxter. "In fact, I don't think any of those were joint jobs. That arrangement was really mostly confined to outright sales."

"I see," said Hazlerigg. "Now about the keys—"

"Well, you're quite right there, too, of course. House agents do hold the keys in nine cases out of ten. It's one of the risks you have to take. We're as careful as we can be in picking our assistants. I've just got my son here and one other, and I'd go bail for both of them. But in a big firm like—well, never mind names. In a big firm, I don't say you mightn't get a bad 'un."

"But so far as you know," said Hazlerigg, "no one person, principal or employer, could have had all the keys on that list."

"You can bet your life on that," agreed Mr. Baxter.

And yet the idea was there.

It was based on something that he had seen or heard when he was completing arrangements for the lease of his own flat. Hazlerigg knew better than to try to force these ideas. Instead, he went home early and had a good night's rest.

It was on the top of the bus, on his way to Scotland Yard next morning, that it clicked.

As soon as he reached his office he got on the telephone to Mr. Rumbold of Wragg and Rumbold, Solicitors.

"Can you tell me," he said, "when you acted for me in the lease of my flat – what did we get?"

"What do you mean?" said Mr. Rumbold cautiously.

"What papers did we get? I seem to remember signing a document of some sort which had to be handed over. Did we get anything in exchange?"

"You signed a counterpart lease," said Mr. Rumbold, "and received the original lease for yourself."

"Have you got it there?"

"It's in my strong-room," said Mr. Rumbold.

"Then get it out, please," said Hazlerigg. "I'm coming round to see you."

Half an hour later he was in Mr. Rumbold's office in Goleman Street, and he and his solicitor were examining an engrossment.

"Is there anything that strikes you as unusual about this lease?" asked Hazlerigg.

Mr. Rumbold picked up the four pages of heavy parchment, folded bookwise, and ran a conveyancer's eye over them.

"No," he said at last. "There's certainly nothing irregular about it, if that's what you mean. In fact," he went on, "it's rather a conscientious piece of work."

"Rather unusually conscientious?"

"By present-day standards, perhaps, yes. It has a large-scale plan, showing each individual room – that is perhaps a little uncommon in a lease of house property."

"And that schedule thing?"

"Most leases of furnished flats have schedules of contents," said Mr.

Rumbold. "Then if any question of dilapidations arises—"

Hazlerigg ran his eye down the schedule.

"One sideboard with two drawers and two cupboards (locked)," he saw. This appeared to decide him.

"Look here," he said. "Can you get hold of some of the other leases of flats on this list?"

"Well—yes. I might," said Mr. Rumbold. "I think I acted for Mrs. Frobisher myself – and Colonel Davenant goes to Lathoms – they'd lend me the lease if I gave some reason."

"Make up anything you like," said Hazlerigg. "I promise you your professional reputation won't be compromised. But collect as many of them as you can."

"It'll take a bit of time."

"One other thing," said Hazlerigg. "When you'd actually completed the arrangements for my lease, you yourself handed me the keys. That was the fact that stuck in my memory. Now, how did you get them? What was the routine? Who gave them to you?"

"The solicitors on the other side, I should imagine," said Mr. Rumbold. "They handed them over at completion."

"Is that usual?"

"In the sale of a freehold property, yes. In the lease of a flat it's more usual, perhaps, for the house agent to hand them direct to the incoming tenant."

"But a solicitor is perfectly within his rights in asking for them, so that he can hand them over himself?"

"Certainly, yes. I should say that was the proper way to do it."

"I see," said Hazlerigg. As, indeed, he was beginning to.

Mr. Rumbold was better than his word. Two days later he had six leases spread out on his desk when Hazlerigg called. He was examining them with the beginnings of a frown on his plump face.

"There's no doubt about it," he said, in answer to the Inspector's first question. "They were all drawn by the same man. As you know, a solicitor doesn't actually put his name on an engrossment, but there are so many points of similarity. You see – the same large-scale plan. The same detailed schedules of furniture. But it isn't only that. Look at that last clause—"

When Hazlerigg had deciphered the script he threw back his head and laughed aloud.

"Genius," he said. "That's genius – the genuine unmistakable touch. Now for it. Who drew these leases?"

"That's an easy one to answer," said Mr. Rumbold. "If the same firm acted for all the landlords, I can find them by turning up your file. Incidentally, that explains the agents, too. If we're dealing here with only two or three groups of landlords or estate corporations who employ the same solicitor, they would naturally use the same two or three agents – there's usually some sort of professional tie-up." He was opening the file as he spoke.

"Henryman and Bosforth," he said. "I don't know much about them. Their office is just off Bedford Row."

A little later that morning Inspector Hazlerigg was shown into the outer office of Henryman and Bosforth. Inspector Pickup was just behind him, and Sergeant Crabbe loitered unobtrusively on the opposite pavement.

"It's about the lease of my flat," he said to the girl. "Start and Baxter of Hornsey are the agents. They told me—"

"Oh, yes," said the girl. "That'll be our Mr. Copley. He does all that. Would you wait in here for a moment? I'll send him down. Are you—? "

"The other gentleman is with me," said Hazlerigg vaguely.

They sat in the small waiting room. Five minutes passed.

"You don't think he's walked out on us, do you?" said Pickup anxiously.

"Grabbe will pick him up if he has," said Hazlerigg. "There's only one way out. No, here he comes."

There was the sound of light footsteps tripping down the stairs and a little man came almost dancing in. Just inside the door hung a huge framed advertisement of the Consequential Insurance Company, its glass shining. As he passed it the little man paused for a moment to straighten his perfectly straight tie.

"Gentlemen," he said, "I am Mr. Copley. I am very glad to see you."

"Mr. Copley," said Inspector Hazlerigg, "you are not nearly as glad to see me" —Pickup slid unobtrusively between him and the door— "as I am to see you . . ."

I heard the whole story from Inspector Hazlerigg some time later.

"What was it you spotted in the leases? What did they all have in common?" I asked.

"Well, it wasn't a pinch of dust," said Hazlerigg.

"All right," I said, "don't rub it in. What was it?"

"They all had a clause," said Hazlerigg, "forbidding the tenant to keep a dog."

The King in Pawn

The Queen's Own Royal South London Rifles has its depot in Southwark High Street and has long recruited both its regular and territorial regiments from the young toughs who live thereabouts. How Detective Inspector Petrella became an honorary member of this excellent regiment and a welcome guest at its functions is a story which has never been fully or truthfully told.

It started on a blustery evening in March. It had been a tiresome day. There had been a case of shoplifting, rendered more unpleasant than usual by the fact that children had been trained to do the stealing; there had been three larcenies from parked cars, a case of organised pocket-picking in a bus queue and, that the measure should be pressed down and overflowing, a little matter of defalcation from the police canteen at Gabriel Street itself.

"Is everyone incurably dishonest?" said Petrella to Superintendent Benjamin.

"Lucky the canteen fiddle wasn't one of our boys," said Benjamin. "I never trusted that civilian caterer."

"Most of the people we've had in today didn't need the money. Not really need it. Those dreadful women, smoking like chimneys, dressed up to the nines, training their own kids to lift stuff—"

"Opportunity," said Benjamin, "makes crime. Cut down the opportunities, you'll cut the crime. You know who I'd like to put inside, Patrick? Receivers. Shut one of them up and you stop a hundred crimes that haven't been committed."

Petrella had heard all this before and knew it to be true. But it had been too hard a day for easy optimism.

"Receivers are like the hydra," he said. "Cut off one head, and a hundred more spring up."

"Little men," said Benjamin. "You're talking about little men. People who'll hide a carton of stolen cigarettes in the washtub and sweat every time the doorbell goes. I'm not talking about little men, Patrick. I'm talking about the two or three who matter. You know you did your best job the first month you were here, when you ran in old Bonny. Pick up the King, and you can claim your pension."

Pick up the King, thought Petrella, as he left Gabriel Street that evening. He had one more call to make, in the Pardoe Street area, and then he was going home. Pick up the King. It sounded easy, when you said it. And some day, no doubt, somebody would do it. Even the smartest criminals made a mistake in the end. But the King had had a very long run.

His name had been spoken in South London for twenty years or more. It had been whispered among informers, the little spreading grass roots of the underworld.

The King was older than the oldest detective in X Division. He dealt in jewellery, in precious stones, and metals of all sorts. So much was known.

A man who pulled a job of this sort had only to wait for a telephone call. Sooner or later it would come. Be at a certain place at a certain time. The place was somewhere, anywhere, in South London. The time was after dark. A car would draw up, a gloved hand hold out a packet of notes. The same hand would receive the parcel of stolen goods. The car would drive off.

There was no pause to check the jewellery; no time to count the notes. Each side trusted the other because, in the long run, it paid them to do so. Just once, soon after the war ended, Big Lewis had the idea of substituting a packet of inferior stones for the diamonds he had lifted from Gurlier's. The real diamonds he had retained at home under a loose tile in the kitchen, with an eye to disposing of them subsequently at even greater profit. When he got home he found three plainclothes men waiting for him. They knew about the loose tile, too. The King was as quick as that.

79

It was from Big Lewis, who realised he had been shopped, that the police had most of their information about the King. It amounted to precious little. It was clearly a waste of time trying to trace him through the cars he used, for these would be 'borrowed' from a car park, and returned without the owners ever being aware of the use to which their property had been put. It was a method which left remarkably few loose ends.

The name itself might have some significance. In the curious warped humour of the underworld "names might have two or even three meanings. (Had there not been another famous receiver known as Treble Eleven, who turned out to be a middle-aged paperseller, a woman named Poppy?)

Petrella had his own ideas about the King. He thought maybe they were dealing with a dynasty. Not one King, but a line of Kings. The stock-in-trade of such a man was knowledge. Knowing who would be likely to pull certain jobs. Knowing the disgruntled deckhands and too-clever airline operatives who would carry the stuff out of the country; knowing the buyers in Paris and Amsterdam; knowing how to get the end money back to England. When the reigning King had made his pile, what was to prevent him disposing of this knowhow to a carefully chosen successor?

"A hydra," said Petrella. "A dynasty of hydras."

It was at this point in his reflections that a heavy brass ashtray came sailing through a window close to his right cheek, covered him with splintered glass, ricocheted from a lamp post and came to rest in the gutter with a sullen clang.

Petrella shook the glass carefully out of his raincoat while he considered the matter.

The window through which the ashtray had come belonged, he saw, to the private bar of a small public house, the Kentish Giant. He was aware of raised voices and stamping feet within. There came a further crash, a progression of crashes as though a child was dragging the cloth off a dinner table laid for twelve.

Petrella opened the door and looked inside.

The fight was almost over.

In the middle of the room a subsiding group was composed of a stout man in shirtsleeves, a youth in an apron, a man in a blue suit, and a man in denim overalls. All of them were holding on to outlying portions of a fifth man, a large man with a red face, a shock of close-cropped hair, and a morosely pugnacious expression.

The large man heaved like a balloon at its guide ropes. His captors held firm. A steady flow of obscenity rose from all five; rose, mingled, and ascended with the dust of their stamping.

Petrella stepped cautiously past the overturned table and through the litter of broken glasses on the floor.

"Lay off, now," said the stout man in shirtsleeves. "Lay off, do you hear, or we'll do you proper."

The red-faced man said an unprintable word and stamped on the stout man's toe. The group swayed dangerously.

"Stop it!" said Petrella.

The note of authority was unmistakable. He added formally, "I'm a detective inspector, and I shall have to take you" —he addressed the red-faced man— "into custody for occasioning a breach of the peace."

"You take him right away," agreed the man in shirtsleeves. "Come in here, busting up my place, eh?"

"That's right," said the youth. It seemed to be the general view.

Petrella said, "Come with me."

The man, unconstrained but unsupported, swayed on his feet and blinked at him.

"Right away," said Petrella. He stepped up close, seized the man's forearm just above the elbow, and started to push. Surprisingly, the man came.

There was no reason for him to do so. By any computation he was stronger and bigger than Petrella. But the fight seemed to be out of him. All the same, Petrella was relieved to meet a pair of patrolling policemen at the first corner.

He went with them to Southwark Police Station and saw to the formalities. The red-faced man, who gave his name as Albert Porter, retired to the cells.

Petrella went home.

81

Before he went into Court next morning, he found time for a word with the landlord of the Kentish Giant.

"Albert's all right," said the landlord. "Generally, he's quite all right. I've known him for years. So have the boys. Don't know what came over him last night."

The landlord's son said, "Before he started busting the place up he was on about that business of his, you know, the garage."

"I heard he'd been led up the old garden path," said the landlord. "Something he put his money into when he came out of the army. Maybe that's what set him off. I expect that was it. Funny thing, I've known it happen before. Like Jock Andrews. Lost his wife, brooded over it. Came in about a month later, had a couple of pints – not more than a couple of pints – and started breaking up the happy home."

Petrella steered the conversation back to Albert Porter.

"He was in the South Londons," said the landlord's son. "Company Sergeant Major. *My* Sergeant Major."

His voice had the disillusion of youth misled. Petrella sympathised with him. A tragedy in the Greek fashion. The godlike figure of the parade ground and the barrack hut reduced to a red-faced, brawling nuisance.

"He had his troubles," said the landlord, "like I said. Came out two years ago when they were thinning 'em out and paying 'em off. Officers and N.C.O.s. Albert took what was coming to him and put it in a garage. Diddun turn out well."

"I see," said Petrella. It seemed to him a remote reason for breaking up a friendly public house. "You'll probably both have to give evidence."

"Wooden want to do that," said the landlord.

Fortunately there was no need for anyone to give evidence.

Albert Porter, revived by his night in the cells and spruced up in a way known only to ex-sergeant majors, stood four-square in the box and pleaded guilty.

Petrella told his story, leaning heavily on the side of mitigation, and the prisoner was bound over.

Petrella caught up with him as he was leaving the court and said,

"Come and have a cup of tea. I want to hear about your garage."

Mr. Porter looked at Petrella doubtfully, then grunted and said, "I've told so many people about it, another can't hurt, I suppose."

"I'll pay for the tea," said Petrella. "You talk."

It was a sad story, but not a new one. Ex-Sergeant Major Porter, with two thousand pounds burning a hole in his pocket, had met Mr. Morris. Mr. Morris was a respectable citizen. At fifty yards on a foggy night he was still a respectable citizen. A pillar of an unspecified church, a member of the local Chamber of Commerce. The source of Mr. Morris's wealth and respectability was the Rampart Garage.

"The Rampart?" said Petrella. "Yes, of course I know it. Corner of Buckingham Road. I've often stopped there for a couple of gallons myself."

"It's a lovely business," said Porter. "No fooling, a lovely business. Big repair shed. Lot of concessions for branded goods. Steady oil and petrol sales. Ol' Morris said he was aiming to get out gradually. Offered me a quarter share for two thousand pounds *and* a job. I've done a lot of work on engines. I started life in the R.E.M.E. It seemed to be just the job."

"So you paid down your money," said Petrella, "without getting a lawyer or an accountant to vet the proposition first, and you discovered the snag when it was too late to do anything about it. Right?"

Mr. Porter nodded.

"What *was* the snag, by the way?"

"It's going to be pulled down. Road widening."

"I see. All the same—" Petrella considered. "If the local authority acquire the site and pull down the garage, they'll have to pay compensation. Good compensation. You'll get a quarter of that."

"Not me. The bank's got a mortgage on the place. For more than the compensation."

"What about all the gear?"

"The pumps and stuff belong to the oil company. They've got a mortgage on the place, too; there's an awful lot of other stuff but I doubt if it'll fetch a thousand pounds at knockdown prices."

"I see," said Petrella.

"The site's the real value of the place. The site and the connection. Once they've gone, there's nothing left. I paid two thousand pounds for nothing. That's the short and the long of it. And there's nothing anyone can do about it."

"Maybe," said Petrella. "Maybe not."

He spent half an hour that afternoon with a dry but helpful little man in the office of the local planning authority, who unrolled the planning map and confirmed that the Rampart Garage was indeed due to disappear.

"The real trouble," he said, "is Palace Crescent. It's residential, and packed with private cars. That means there's a constant flow of traffic where we least want it – here." He put his thumb down, a modern Roman Emperor condemning a full arena. "Where it runs out into the main road. And the garage is right on the corner. It is the corner site."

"That's right," said Petrella. "That's what makes it such a marvellous place for a garage."

"It'll be a year or more before we get going on that bit. And when we do acquire it, your friend will get compensation."

"Nothing like enough, I'm afraid," said Petrella.

He said it absent-mindedly. For an idea had come to him. A wild, splendid, mad idea. An idea of curious ramifications and infinite possibilities; and he wanted time to look at it.

He made some excuses, got out of the council offices, and walked back in the direction of the Rampart Garage.

A café across the street offered a handy observation point. He took a cup of tea to a table by the window. Business at the garage was brisk. In the first half-hour he counted twenty cars in and out.

The petrol pumps, which Albert was serving, stood in a forecourt at the point of the angle made by the two roads. Behind them stood the garage block, with a main drive-in entrance for cars, and a glass door on the right leading to an office. Behind that again was an area of repair shops. The whole thing was one of those confused, casual, but workable jumbles calculated to infuriate any right-minded planner.

At the end of the half-hour his patience was rewarded. The office door opened and Mr. Morris came out. Petrella felt sure that it was Mr.

Morris: a man of about sixty-five, stocky, bright-eyed, rosy-cheeked, sporting a short but aggressive white beard. He stood for a moment, eyeing the hurrying traffic as his Norse ancestor might have stood at the prow of his longship surveying potential victims.

He said something to Albert. They still seemed to be on friendly terms. Petrella was surprised at this, but reflected that in Albert's place he would probably have done the same. The closer he stuck to the garage, the closer he stayed by his own two thousand pounds.

It was at this point that the idea he had had earlier on was enlarged. It ceased to be nebulous, and became concrete. He paid his bill and went back to Gabriel Street.

"Go to a lawyer?" said Albert. "Throw good money after bad? I ought to have gone to one to start with, there I agree with you. But it can't do any good now. He hasn't broken any law that I know of."

"Try it," said Petrella.

"Don't know any lawyers."

"I know lots," said Petrella. He considered the solicitors with whom he had had dealings, and selected Mr. Trapper as most appropriate to this problem. "And what's more I'll come with you."

"You think it'll do any good?"

"I've got an idea. Until we've talked it over with someone who knows the ropes, I can't tell if it's any good or not."

"Might as well try it," said Albert.

Mr. Trapper had an office near the Oval cricket ground. He was big, heavy, full-jowled and had hair so strong and so black that he never looked properly shaved. He called Petrella 'Patrick', greeted Albert kindly, listened to his story, and perused the contents of the envelope of papers that he had brought along with him.

"He certainly did the thing in style," said Mr. Trapper. "That's old Morris who owns the Rampart, isn't it? Chap with a beard. Looks like a regular old pirate."

"All I can say is, it looked all right at the time," said Albert.

"Nice little business, I should have said. What's the catch? Oh,

85

planning trouble."

Petrella explained about the planning trouble. Mr. Trapper listened to him carefully, but continued reading the papers at the same time, a facility that busy lawyers seem to acquire.

"Hullo," he said. "What's this? You didn't tell me he'd given you a debenture on the place."

Albert took the proffered document cautiously and said, "That's right. A debenture. A sort of mortgage, isn't it?"

"Yes and no," said Mr. Trapper. "It's a mortgage in so far as it gives you a charge on the place. Well, that's not much good because the bank and the petrol company have got charges in front of you, if you follow me?"

"In a way," said Mr. Porter.

"But it gives you other remedies, as well. For instance, this entitles you to six per cent on your money, payable monthly. Have you had that?"

"What I get from Morris is my wages. Twelve pounds a week, and he takes the P.A.Y.E. off himself before he pays 'em."

"In that case," said Mr. Trapper, folding his massive black hairy hands on the desk, "your debenture interest is clearly in arrears. You should at once appoint a receiver."

The word hung in the dusty office.

"A receiver?" said Petrella.

"Not the sort of receiver you're thinking of, Patrick. A legal receiver. Any debenture holder or mortgagee has that remedy."

"What does a receiver do?"

"He takes charge," said Mr. Trapper briskly. "His authority will be supported, if necessary, by the Court. He receives all rents, controls the bank account, runs the business, makes an inventory of the stock, and he arranges for periodical checks and audits."

"Can he exclude the proprietor?"

"If it was the proprietor who granted the debenture, certainly. It might be his duty to exclude him. Prevent him tampering with the assets."

"Do you" —as Petrella spoke he was conscious of a fierce and unhallowed joy as his idea fulfilled itself— "do you *know* any receivers?"

"Oh, dozens of 'em. Accountants mostly. I think Bowles would be the man for you here."

"How do we appoint him?"

"Just sign a document I'll draw up for you. What's today? Friday. I'll get Bowles on the telephone. Give him a day to get organised. I suggest he goes in on Monday."

"Mr. Morris is rather an explosive personality," said Petrella. "He might try to make things a bit hot for Mr. Bowles. You'd better warn him."

"Bowles is quite capable of looking after himself," said Mr. Trapper.

On Monday morning, as was his custom, Mr. Morris arrived at the Rampart Garage at nine o'clock sharp. Petrella had been at his observation post in the café for half an hour. He wanted to see the curtain go up.

The first big moment arrived when Mr. Morris found that the office door was not only locked, but apparently bolted, too. He walked round and put his nose up against the window, from which a light was showing. Then he rapped on the window and shouted something through it.

Petrella paid his bill, went out, crossed the street higher up, and drifted back towards the garage. As he reached the corner, the door was opened and a tall thin man, wearing steel spectacles, peered out.

"Are you Mr. Morris?" he enquired.

"That's right. I am," said Mr. Morris. "And who the flame something-or-other are you?"

"My name," said the tall man severely, "is Bowles. I am a receiver, placed in possession of the premises by your debenture holder, Mr. Porter. This is a copy of the instrument appointing me. The original has been filed with the Registrar of Companies."

Mr. Morris made a monosyllabic and, on the whole, improbable suggestion about the Registrar of Companies.

"If you have any proper communication to make," said Mr. Bowles, "might I suggest you make it in writing?" He started to close the door again. Mr. Morris got his foot into it.

"You let me in at once," he said, "or I'll call a policeman. Keeping a man out of his own office."

"There is a policeman on the corner," said Mr. Bowles. "In fact, I fancy he is coming this way now."

Petrella withdrew discreetly. He was inclined to agree with Mr. Trapper that Bowles could look after himself.

So began the siege of the Rampart.

It lasted, in all, for three days. Petrella saw some of it, and heard the rest from Albert who continued to serve oil and petrol to customers unconscious of the drama that was being played around them.

The policeman had apparently decided in favour of Mr. Bowles. Mr. Morris had withdrawn, no doubt to consult his own solicitor. Not finding much comfort in the law, he had decided on a dawn attack, and had arrived, on Tuesday morning, at eight o'clock. Anticipating this, Mr. Bowles had arrived at half past seven.

In the lunch interval Mr. Morris had sought out Albert.

"Really very nice to me, too," said Albert. "Stood me my lunch, and all. Of course, I told him it wasn't in my hands, really. He ought to approach me through my solicitors. Then he said some things about solicitors. Would have done you good to hear him."

"Keep it up," said Petrella. He thought for a moment and added, "I'll tell you what. Suggest to Bowles that he ought to start making an inventory. All the old stuff in that repair shop and the store shed."

"It'd take him a month of Sundays."

"I don't think he'll actually have to do it. But let Mr. Morris hear about it. Tell him that Bowles has been asking you for the keys of the different lockers and boxes. Tell him that if he doesn't get them, he's going to start breaking them open. I *think* that ought to do the trick."

On Wednesday, in the early afternoon, Albert telephoned Petrella.

"Worked a treat," he said. "He's going to pay up."

"I thought he might," said Petrella.

"Interest, and everything. As long as I get Bowles out by tea time."

"Fine," said Petrella. "Of course, it won't do him a lot of good. Because if you withdraw your receiver and take your money, the bank or the petrol company could probably put him in again."

"I think he knows that," said Albert. "He's been to his lawyer, too. He doesn't seem to care. What he said was, as long as Bowles is out by tea time, I can have my money."

"And what does Bowles say?"

"As soon as Morris has paid me, he's got to go. Of course, as you say, he might be put back again by one of the others, but it'd take a bit of time."

"All right," said Petrella. "That's fine." And he meant it.

He went round to Division and had a word with Superintendent Benjamin. "It's still a long shot," he said. "But the odds are shortening."

"Four cars," said Benjamin. "No – five. We don't want any slip-up now. One crew to block each of the roads, and one in reserve."

"We could observe from the café," said Petrella. "The proprietor's got an upstairs room he'd let us use. And a telephone—"

Much electricity was consumed that night at the Rampart Garage. From their vantage point over the way, Benjamin and Petrella could follow Mr. Morris's progress by the switching on and off of lights, from front office to back office, from back office to storeroom, from storeroom to repair shop and garage.

"Having a regular spring clean," said Benjamin. "How long's he going to be?"

"He'll be out before daylight," said Petrella.

The superintendent acknowledged this with a grin which had very little humour in it.

At five different points in the streets outside the garage, police cars stood, parked inconspicuously – one man dozing at the wheel, one man in the back, one man alert for the signal.

It was close on two o'clock in the morning when Petrella said, "I think he's coming now, sir."

The big garage doors creaked open. The lights inside were all out now. The length of Buckingham Road lay empty under its glaring orange lamps.

For a moment Mr. Morris stood there as Petrella had seen him stand once before, head forward, white beard jutting. Then he disappeared. Sidelights came on. A big old-fashioned saloon car nosed out into the forecourt.

As Mr. Morris climbed down and went to shut the garage doors behind him, Superintendent Benjamin was talking on the telephone.

"Blue fabric four-door saloon," he said. "Coming now."

Then things started to happen; the saloon car turned right, out of the garage.

Mr. Morris saw the police car draw out at the same time to block the road, slammed his own car into reverse, turned in a savage half circle, and started up one of the side streets. He spotted the second car too late.

As Petrella ran out of the café he heard the scream of brakes and the noise of the impact.

Mr. Morris was still fighting, screaming, a high thin scream, and fighting like a lunatic with two of the patrol-car men. The sergeant stood, a dripping crimson handkerchief to his face.

"Steady," said Petrella. "Steady. He's an old man."

"He's an old bastard," said the sergeant. "Went for my eyes."

"We want him in one piece," said Petrella.

The screaming had stopped now. Mr. Morris was lying on his back on the pavement, bubbling gently and dribbling into his beard. Petrella thought that the bubbling was worse than the screaming.

Three evenings later, in the detective room at Gabriel Street, Superintendent Benjamin straightened his back and said, "That's the lot. All identified. Do you know, he had the bits and pieces of twenty different jewel robberies in that car?"

"Hidden," said Petrella, "I don't doubt, in twenty most ingenious places round that garage. It took *him* eight hours to get them all out, and *he* knew where to look."

"It's magnificent," said Benjamin. He was not a man given to enthusiasm, and when he used a word like magnificent it sounded like an accolade. "There's no doubt about it. We've got our hands on the King at last. We've been so busy in the last three days I haven't even had time to ask you how you spotted him."

"Part hunch," said Petrella. "A garage owner and second hand car man seemed just right. Plenty of excuse to keep ready money about, plenty of hiding-places, and you have to know something about cars if you're going to knock them off. But really it was the joke."

"Joke?"

"You know what they're like round here. A man living at the corner of Buckingham Road and Palace Crescent. What else *could* they call him?"

He looked at his watch and said, "I've got to run. A date with the sergeants and warrant officers of the South Londons. We're celebrating Albert's return to solvency."

The Rich Man in his Castle

When two people fall out and decide to seek legal advice over their dispute, it may seem surprising to you that they should both go to the same firm of solicitors. It is only superficially surprising. For if both of them have used the same firm for a long time, neither may see any reason why he should go elsewhere to oblige the other party. After all, they can always consult different partners. And anyway, in a small country town, there may only *be* one good firm. This may explain why the offices of Messrs. Lamplough, Fairchild and Britt recently received visits, on successive mornings, both from Mr. Snuggs and Sir Charles Pellat.

These offices occupy an early Georgian building in the little square behind the Cornmarket. The brass plate is so worn with age and elbow-grease that the names on it are almost illegible. No one living can remember Mr. Lamplough. There is a portrait of him in the waiting room which exhibits a crop of benevolent mutton-chop whiskers. If you look very closely you can see the rat-trap mouth behind them. Mr. Cyprian Fairchild, the senior partner, is the grandson of the original Fairchild, and is himself approaching retiring age. Older clients value his advice. They realise that he may not be entirely *au fait* with the complexities of modern legislation, but look on him as an old friend and a man of the world. The younger generation of lawyers in the office, headed by the junior partner, Mr. Roger Britt, privately consider him a fuddy-duddy.

Mr. Snuggs parked his brand new three-litre Austin across the backs of two smaller cars, neatly blocking their exits, entered the office with the deliberate tread which befitted an independent tradesman and a man of property and was shown up to the first floor room of young Mr. Britt.

"It's the roof, at the front," said Mr. Snuggs. "Not the new bit over the back extension. That's perfect, and will be for another fifty years."

"It should be," said Mr. Britt, "seeing what it cost your landlord to put it up."

"He could afford it," said Mr. Snuggs. "No. It's the front bit. Two tiles off in the gale last week, and Alfred and Henry ran a ladder up yesterday, and stripped off a few more tiles. We found just what we expected. Wet rot."

Mr. Britt said, 'Tchk, tchk," and made a note. He reflected that it was the fourth such discovery that Mr. Snuggs and his sons had made in the past few years. The others had been dry rot, rising damp, and woodworm. All had been rectified, at considerable expense, by their long-suffering landlord, Sir Charles Pellat.

"Did you mention it to Sir Charles?"

"I did."

"I don't suppose he was pleased."

"He was upset," said Mr. Snuggs, complacently. "But I told him, it's your property. You've got to keep it in repair. Roof and main timbers. That's what the lease says, isn't it?"

"That's roughly correct. Of course, he did build on that rear extension for you three years ago. That was an improvement. He didn't *have* to do that."

"He was improving his own property. It'll come back to him when we go. He may not get it himself. He's an old man. But it'll come back to his family, won't it?"

"That's roughly correct."

"Then he's just investing his own money in his own property."

"That's certainly one way of looking at it," said Mr. Britt. "Did he agree to do the repair?"

"What he said was, seeing as me and my two boys were all builders, why didn't we do it ourselves. Well, I wasn't falling for that. I said, 'We don't mix business with pleasure, Sir Charles. We'd rather get an outside firm to do it, then we'd know the job would be done properly.'

I suggested Palmers."

Mr. Britt made another note. He knew that Palmers were the most expensive builders in the district. He didn't think that Sir Charles would be very pleased. He fancied that they would be seeing him quite soon.

This prediction was promptly fulfilled. At eleven o'clock on the following morning an aged Rolls-Royce pulled into the square and parked across the back of three smaller cars.

Sir Charles was tall and thin. He still retained, in his walk and his talk, a ghost of the cavalry subaltern he had been in the First World War. He refused a seat, and stood beside the fine bow window of Mr. Cyprian Fairchild's ground floor office.

"It's that damned fellow Snuggs," he said.

"At it again, is he?"

"He never stops. Why the devil I ever let him have the lodge, I don't know."

"When your lodge-keeper left, you had to let it to someone."

"Should have chosen an old lady. A nice old lady. Not a bounder like Snuggs."

"You couldn't tell."

"Might have known. Fellow's a builder. Bound to be a crook. They all are."

"That's a bit sweeping," said Mr. Fairchild. "There are honest builders. You happen to have struck a bad 'un, that's all. What does he want now?"

"He wants a new front roof. Cost five hundred pounds. Got the estimate here."

"How much did you pay for that back extension?"

"Fifteen hundred. That was three years ago. Cost more now. And that's on top of what I paid for rebuilding the whole chimney and putting in new casement windows downstairs. To say nothing of regular annual repairs. I calculated the other day" —Sir Charles fished a scrap of paper out of his waistcoat pocket— "that lodge has cost me the thick end of five thousand pounds since the Snuggs went in."

"I suppose it's an investment," said Mr. Fairchild gloomily.

"Investment! Who for? Me? Snuggs and his two great idle sons? I've got no heir, apart from my sister Lucretia, and she's got all the money she wants. And anyway what sort of investment is it, for God's sake? The place must be the best fitted-out cottage in England by now. Worth seven or eight thousand pounds at least. If I had that money invested, I'd get — never was much good at sums."

"At six per cent, you'd get four hundred and eighty pounds a year."

"And the rent I get is thirty-five shillings a week. How much is that a year?"

"Just over ninety pounds."

"Well, there you are," said Sir Charles. He glowered out of the window at a lady driver who was trying with little chance of success to back her car out past his Rolls.

"The trouble is," said Mr. Fairchild, "that *if* you want to sell the Manor House, and I gather you've more or less wholly made up your mind —"

"Got to. Can't keep it up. Barn of a place. Far too big."

"The park's let to an agricultural tenant. So the rent of that's regulated. And the lodge is the only cottage left. If you'd been able to give vacant possession of that, it would have been a great attraction. I wonder if we could buy the Snuggses out."

"They wouldn't go," said Sir Charles. He was staring gloomily out of the window. The woman driver had abandoned the attempt, and started blowing her horn. Sir Charles ignored her. He swung round suddenly, and said, "Do you suppose he'd do a swap?"

Mr. Fairchild gaped at him.

"Do a *what*?" he said.

"A swap. An exchange. I'll take the lodge. He can have the Manor House. *And* the park."

"He can't mean it," said young Mr. Britt.

"He's quite serious. He reckons he'd be much better off in the lodge. He'll be able to save his income instead of spending it trying to keep up the Manor. And he'll be much warmer in winter."

"But what will the Snuggses *do* with the Manor House?"

95

"They're builders, aren't they? Plenty of scope for them."

"It's quite mad," said Mr. Britt. "But all the same—"

"Squire Snuggs," said Mr. Fairchild with a chuckle.

"Think how he'll enjoy that. There are one or two details. Sir Charles would like to keep the shooting. And there's one particularly nice walk, up the beech avenue to that summer-house – on the knoll behind the plantation – a gazebo is the correct name for it, I believe – he'd like to keep a right of way up to that. I'll leave the conveyancing details to you, my boy. It shouldn't take long to fix up."

It took a month to fix up. And Mr. Snuggs seemed happy with the exchange for nearly a year. At the end of that time, he called by appointment to see Mr. Britt, and brought his two sons with him, solid youths, who sat on the edges of their chairs holding their hats in their hands. Mr. Snuggs did most of the talking.

"It's like this," he said, "I want to put things back to what they was before."

"You mean you want to re-exchange the properties?"

"That's right. I want to put it back like it was." His two sons nodded their sombre approval.

"But why?"

"Because it won't work. First, we get no money out of it. What that farmer chap pays us goes on *his* improvements, and anything that's left, goes on rates. Do you know how much the rates are on the Manor?"

"*I* know," said Mr. Britt, "and so do you. Because I told you when you bought it."

"Well, you may have told me, but I didn't take it in. Then there's the repairs. All right, we do them ourselves. But it's bloody hard work—" His two sons nodded emphatically. It was clear to Mr. Britt that most of the hard work was done by them. *"And* it means we can't take on much outside work, so we've got no money coming in. And last but not least – there's the lodge."

"Ah," said Mr. Britt. "The lodge. Yes."

"Twice already this year he's been at us for money. First it was all the guttering wanted redoing. Three hundred pounds that cost us. I offered to do it myself."

"What did he say to that?"

"He said he didn't like to see us mixing business with pleasure. He'd get Palmers to do it."

"Aren't they apt to be a bit expensive?"

"Expensive! They build their houses with gold bricks. Then there was the drains. *We* never found anything wrong with the drains, did we?"

Alfred and Henry shook their heads in unison.

"There was a surveyor's report. I remember."

"Oh yes. He got a surveyor's report all right. Six hundred pounds that cost us. And what are we getting for it? I'll tell you." Mr. Snuggs thumped the table with a large mahogany fist. "Ninety pounds a year, and everyone laughing at us. Why we can't hardly get in our own gate for the bloody cars round *his* front door. *And* he's bought himself a new Aston Martin."

"It's true," said Sir Charles to Mr. Fairchild, "that I do seem to have become a lot more popular since I moved. In the old days no one seemed keen on coming to dinner with me. I couldn't blame them really. When I had guests we used to eat in the big dining room – the one my grandparents put on when they had a royal visitation. It's got three outside walls, and the central heating system at the Manor is so old-fashioned that although it used a ton of coke a week the pipes never got more than luke-warm. I remember once when I had old Colonel Featherstonehaugh to dinner he took a sip of his burgundy – rather a nice Corton incidentally – and said – his teeth were chattering at the time – 'You know Charles, the only w-w-way you could get this w-w-wine down to room temperature – would be to put a l-l-lump of ice in it.'" Sir Charles laughed heartily, and Mr. Fairchild laughed with him.

"So you're better off now?"

"Oh, we're very snug now. The gas-fired central heating keeps the cottage as warm as toast. Of course, I had to pay for the actual boiler. But I stung my landlord for all the builders' work involved. And what's more, now that I don't need the cellar for coal, I've got most of my wine into it. I wonder, would you care to come up next week and try the Clos de Vougeot? It's settled down nicely."

"I'd love to," said Mr. Fairchild.

Pride, plus a determination not to be proved wrong, enabled Mr. Snuggs to stick it for a further twelve months. Then his Austin, two years old now, and in sad need of a respray, crept into the little square behind the Cornmarket. Mr. Snuggs looked almost as battered as his car. He said to Mr. Britt, "It's no good. It's killing me. Something's got to be done."

"It's got worse, has it?"

"Worse? If it goes on for another six months I'll be bankrupt. And every time I go out of my own front gate, I can see that old devil. He sits in his front window all the time, grinning at me. Except when he takes a stroll up to the summer-house, and sits there grinning at all of us. We've got to stop it."

Mr. Britt nearly said, "There's no law against grinning," and then realised that with Mr. Snuggs in his present frame of mind this might cost him a valuable client. He said, "It's not going to be easy."

"Couldn't we put his rent up?"

"It's a controlled rent. I remember explaining it to you when—"

"Yes, yes," said Mr. Snuggs testily. "You've no call to remind me about that. But I recollect there was something about rates."

"The rateable value."

"If it goes up above a certain figure you can get him out. That's right, isn't it?"

"That's roughly correct."

"It's a lovely little cottage. Beautiful state of repair. Modern drainage. Central heating."

"I seem to remember," said Mr. Britt, "that my partner, Mr. Fairchild, argued all those points most persuasively in front of the rating authority, but between us we succeeded in defeating him."

Mr. Snuggs said, "Tchah," and then, "You're a lawyer, aren't you? Why don't you suggest something, instead of just sitting there making remarks."

"Sir Charles is pretty old. And I heard he hasn't been very well lately."

"I believe that's right," said Mr. Snuggs, looking more cheerful. "His sister's come to look after him. And I saw the doctor's car up there two days ago. Why?"

"A protected tenancy is a personal thing. Not something he can leave to his family—"

"You mean, if he popped off, I'd get the cottage back?"

"That's roughly correct."

It was on a Monday morning in January, sharp with the first frost of the new year, that Mr. Fairchild came into Mr. Britt's room with the news.

"It happened sometime last night," he said. "The old boy must have gone for his usual walk up to the gazebo, and had a stroke when he got there."

"A fatal stroke?"

"Dr. Shuttleworth says, no. It probably paralysed him. By a damnable piece of bad luck his sister was out on one of her do-gooding committees and didn't get home till quite late. She assumed he'd already gone to bed. It wasn't until she went to call him this morning that the alarm was sounded. They searched the grounds and found him."

"Then he died of exposure, sometime during the night?"

"Probably quite quickly, Dr. Shuttleworth says. After a stroke, his vitality would be very low."

"Poor old chap," said Mr. Britt.

Mr. Snuggs, who called on the following day, expressed somewhat different sentiments.

"We've all got to go sometime," he said, concealing any grief he may have felt. "I expect it was as good a way as any. Doctors nowadays keep old people living far too long. If it's right he was paralysed, he wouldn't have enjoyed life, would he? A misery to himself and everyone else."

"I suppose that's right," said Mr. Britt.

"Person I feel most sorry for is that sister of his. She'll have to find somewhere to live. She gave up her own house, you know, when she came to look after him, in the summer. Something wrong?"

"In the summer?" croaked Mr. Britt.

"That's right. Have I said something I shouldn't?"

"Do you – do you happen to remember exactly when?"

"As a matter of fact, I do. It was on Midsummer Day. Longest day of the year. I remember remarking on it to Henry. Look here, Britt, what's all this about?"

"And she's been living at the lodge ever since?"

"That's right. Like I said, he needed a bit of looking after at the end."

"And if she came on Midsummer Day, she's been there more than six months."

"So what?"

Mr. Britt was thumbing feverishly through the stout, olive-green book on his desk.

"It's one of the earlier Rent Acts," he said. "The Act of 1920. Section twelve. That's right. Sub-section one. I'd entirely overlooked the possibility – yes."

"Stop all this money talk," said Mr. Snuggs, his face bright red, "and explain."

Mr. Britt explained.

"You mean," said Mr. Snuggs, when he had finally taken it in, "that because she's a relative, and because she's lived there more than six months, I can't turn *her* out either."

"That's roughly correct."

A gleam of hope appeared in Mr. Snuggs' watery eyes. "Perhaps she don't know about this old Act," he said.

"It's a possibility. But when I saw her coming out of Mr. Fairchild's room this morning I remember thinking she looked remarkably cheerful.

"Perhaps if I offered her something—"

"You could try," said Mr. Britt.

He had only met Miss Pellat once, but she had struck him as a remarkably tough character.

Mr. Snuggs tried that afternoon. He found Miss Lucretia Pellat in the small but nicely furnished front room of the lodge, pouring out tea from a heavy old silver pot. He refused the offer of a cup for himself and opened his proposition.

Miss Pellat shook her head. She shook it so emphatically that her long jade earrings tinkled.

"I wouldn't dream of moving," she said. "It's a dear little house. Full of memories of the happy times my dear brother had here. He *was* happy, you know."

"I dare say he was," said Mr. Snuggs morosely.

"He kept his health to the last. When Providence delivered that final stroke, I could not help thinking that it was a perfect ending. Provided" — and on the word Miss Pellat leaned forward so sharply that her earrings tinkled again— "provided that it killed him."

"Well, it did," said Mr. Snuggs.

"That's not true. It was the night in the open that killed him. If I had summoned help, and had him carried back to the house – taken to a hospital or nursing home – injected with drugs, no doubt he could have been saved. And saved for what. A pitiful, half-paralysed, old age. Like a mouse, caught by its back legs in a trap. I knew my brother too well to think he would have wanted that."

Mr. Snuggs had got his breath back by now. He said, "Do you mean to say you were with him when it happened and you just left him there to die."

"Death by exposure is quick, and not uncomfortable. If you read the diaries of the great Polar explorers you will find that it comes with a feeling of warmth and relaxation."

Mr. Snuggs stared at her, horrified. "But," he said, "you're his sister. How could you do it? Walk off like that and leave him."

"I didn't walk straight off," said Miss Pellat, and her voice sounded a clear note of warning.

101

"You didn't, eh?"

"Because, when I'd only got as far as the edge of the wood, I heard a car coming. Your car, Mr. Snuggs."

Mr. Snuggs stared at her, hypnotised.

"And I saw you get out, and walk over, and look at my brother. And I saw *you* walk away again."

There was a long, long silence. At last Mr. Snuggs said, in a croaking voice, "I deny it."

"Of course you do. And everything that I told you is entirely – what do the lawyers say – without prejudice. Such a curious expression. No, no, I am sure we can keep each other's little secret, Mr. Snuggs."

As he rose heavily to his feet, she added, "By the way, I fear I shall have to ask you to do something about the bath. I really need an entirely new one. And whilst you're at it, you might let me have a new sink as well—"

Where There's a Will

Malcolm Preece settled himself into the far corner seat of the last first class carriage on the 7.55 a.m. train from Bramhill to London. The seat was one in which long usage had given him almost prescriptive rights. After blowing his nose and wishing his regular travelling companion, Mr. Satterthwaite, "Good morning," he turned to the obituary columns of *The Times*.

A familiar name caught his eye.

"I see one of our local celebrities has gone," he said.

"Not Miss Pringle?" said Mr. Satterthwaite. "Dear, dear, and we all thought she'd make her century."

"No. Not Miss Pringle. Colonel Spender."

"I heard he'd been ill. He was a tough old boy. We thought he might have got over it."

"Not this time," said Mr. Preece and handed his copy of the paper to Mr. Satterthwaite, across a small woman who had presumed to occupy the seat between them. Mr. Preece suspected that she hadn't got a first class ticket.

Spender. Ambrose. After a painful illness gallantly borne. Died in Guildford Infirmary. No flowers. Donations to the Imperial War Graves Commission.

"An eccentric character, by all accounts," said Mr. Satterthwaite.

"He was one of my clients," said Mr. Preece, with a note of reproof.

"Then I withdraw the remark. If he was a client of the firm of Preece and Sexton he must have been a man of the highest repute."

"He had had a rather odd career," conceded Mr. Preece. "He described himself as Colonel Spender. I had been told, in strict confidence" —and here Mr. Preece glared at the small woman as if daring her to repeat something overheard, in confidence, in a first class railway carriage— "that he was awarded this rank, and a number of English and foreign decorations too, for daring Intelligence work behind the enemy lines."

"I only knew him vaguely," said Mr. Satterthwaite. "He had one of those houses in Knap Woods, didn't he? Rather nice houses, but a bit isolated."

"Not exactly isolated. A bit remote."

"Wasn't that where they found that woman – what was her name?"

"Mrs. Slane."

"Mrs. Slane. That's right. She'd been knocked on the head. But not robbed or—er—assaulted. The police never solved it."

"It was a complete mystery," said Mr. Preece, "and it looks like staying that way. It's nearly two years since it happened. The trail must be getting very cold by now."

The small woman, who was tired of being ignored, said defiantly, "My aunt's cook, who was walking out with one of the policemen, told her that the case was *not* closed. They had a clue. And he told her what it was – in confidence, of course."

"Oh?" said Mr. Preece.

"Really?" said Mr. Satterthwaite.

Both gentlemen then retired behind their newspapers and did not utter another word until the train reached Waterloo.

If a certain disparity in temperament produces the happiest marriages, the same might be said of professional partnerships. Certainly the solicitor's practice of Messrs. Preece and Sexton, though not long established in Bedford Row, managed to get along well enough, although it would have been hard to find two men of more widely different characters than Mr. Preece and Mr. Sexton.

Malcolm Preece was correct in dress and deportment, conservative in outlook, and extremely conscientious in his work. He was normally the first to arrive at the office, and often the last to leave. Andrew Sexton was casual, empirical and occasionally, in Mr. Preece's view, unnecessarily flippant. However, it was a combination of talents which seemed to work. As Mr. Preece sometimes remarked to his clients, "If there's a theoretical solution, I can usually work it out. If I'm stuck, Andrew Sexton can often find a practical answer."

Whilst they were opening and sorting out the mail, a ritual which they carried out together every morning, Mr. Preece told Andrew Sexton of the death of Colonel Spender.

"Yes," said Mr. Sexton, "I saw it in *The Times.* I thought I'd get his will up so that we could have a look at it. I believe you're his sole executor, aren't you?"

"I think I am," said Mr. Preece.

He was untwisting the string which held down the flap of the deed wallet. The first things which slid out as he opened it were a long, legal-looking envelope, then a smaller square one.

"That's the will," said Mr. Preece. "What's the other one? I don't remember it."

Mr. Sexton picked it up. On it, neatly typed, were the words, *To be placed with my will, and opened only at my death,* followed by the initials, also typed, *A.S.*

"It has always seemed curious to me," said Mr. Preece, "that people will employ a solicitor to make a perfectly sound will for them, and then clutter it round – hand me that paper knife, would you – with so-called letters of instruction, which are legally ineffective, and, in any event, so woollily drawn that they can't be carried out – good heavens!"

"What is it?"

"I can't believe it. It's not possible."

"What isn't possible?"

"Colonel Spender—no—"

Mr. Sexton grabbed the single sheet of notepaper from his partner's hand, read it, and whistled.

"Well," he said, "the old devil! I knew he was a queer cuss, but this beats everything."

"Do you think it's true? It can't be, can it? It's some sort of joke."

"If you think it's a joke," said Sexton, "the most sensible thing would be to tear it up and forget about it."

"Good heavens, we can't do that. If the colonel took the trouble to leave it with his will, he must have meant me to act on it. As the executor, I've no choice."

"Then you'll have to show it to the police. They'll have to make their minds up what they're going to do. Come to think of it, there's not much they *can* do now, is there?"

"I suppose not," said Mr. Preece thoughtfully. "No."

The typewritten slip was short and to the point. It said, *Theresa Slane was a poisonous bitch. I knocked her on the head and have few regrets. I'm leaving this note with my will in case some other poor devil gets suspected of it. She had plenty of enemies, God knows. Incidentally, if the police don't believe me, ask them whether or not they found an artificial pigskin glove near the body.*

The note was unsigned. The two lawyers were still looking at it when the telephone rang.

So strong is the association of ideas that, even as Mr. Preece stretched out his hand to lift the receiver, he hesitated. "Suppose it's the police," he said. "What am I to say?"

"Why should it be the police?"

"No reason, really, I suppose. No. I'm being stupid."

Mr. Preece lifted the receiver. The girl on the switchboard said, "Oh, Mr. Preece. It's Colonel Spender for you. I'll put you through."

Mr. Preece had just sufficient presence of mind to hand his partner an extension receiver, and both of them listened to the wheezy voice at the other end.

"Thought I'd ring you up," it said. "Just seen *The Times* myself. Thought I'd better explain, in case you jumped to the wrong conclusion. Ambrose Spender's my cousin. Distant cousin. Same name. Soon as I get out of this damned hospital I'll be round to see you. Got one or two things to discuss. Important things. Goodbye for now."

Mr. Preece looked at Mr. Sexton; and Mr. Sexton looked at Mr. Preece. There was a long silence. The younger man recovered his voice first.

"I think we'd better put this back in its envelope, don't you?" he said. "After all, the instructions were that it wasn't to be opened *until*

106

death."

"Pretend we haven't seen it?"

"That's right."

"We can't do that."

"Why not?"

"As an officer of the court . . ." said Mr. Preece.

When he used these words, Mr. Preece, unlike many solicitors, really meant something by them. He saw himself dressed in some undefined but imposing legal uniform, defending the ancient rules and practices of the law against all attackers.

When he heard the fatal words, Mr. Sexton realised that it was no occasion for flippancy. He said, speaking slowly, "If you feel that we can't ignore this information, even though it has come into our hands in an irregular manner – for we had of course no right to open the envelope until we were sure that Colonel Spender was dead – then where do you visualise that our duty lies?"

This was the right approach. Irregularity and duty were words which Mr. Preece understood.

He said, "We shall have to consider our next move very carefully. In my submission, we have a double duty in the matter. A duty to our client not to involve him prematurely. An equally important duty to the public not to suppress vital information about a crime. Indeed, to suppress it entirely would make us guilty of compounding a felony."

"Accessories after the fact?"

"Something of that sort." Like most solicitors whose practices were confined to conveyancing and probate, Mr. Preece really knew very little about the criminal law. "And have you considered that the police are certainly still working on the case? The files on a murder are never closed. Someone was mentioning, only this morning, that they had a clue. Why, they could even be on the point of arresting some innocent person! If we produced this information *after* that happened it would certainly be suspect. We might have manufactured it ourselves. The note is only typed—"

"And on a Remington standard machine," said Mr. Sexton. "We've got half a dozen of them in the office."

"Now that you mention it," said Mr. Preece, "it is even possible that it *was* typed in this office. I recollect that when Colonel Spender came to discuss his will he arrived early for his appointment, and was put in one of the smaller offices which happened to be empty – the waiting room was being redecorated at the time, you remember."

Mr. Sexton examined the note more closely.

"I think you're right," he said. "And what's more, he used a piece of *our* paper. It's that cream-laid quarto that we had a stock of. The girls used to complain that it was so thick they couldn't take a proper carbon copy."

"I've been thinking," said Mr. Preece. "I know the superintendent at Bramhill quite well. In fact, we've played golf together more than once. Suppose that I give him this information, without revealing where it comes from?"

"He's certain to want to know. What will you say when he asks you?"

"It's perfectly simple. I shall say that the source of the information is connected with one of my clients, and is therefore privileged."

"I see," said Mr. Sexton doubtfully. "I hope he remembers he's a friend and not just a policeman."

However, when Mr. Preece presented himself at Bramhill Police Station that evening, he was told that the friendly golf-playing superintendent was on leave, and would be absent for a fortnight. This was disconcerting. He hardly felt that he could withhold vital information so long. He found himself talking to a much younger and less friendly detective inspector.

As soon as Mr. Preece mentioned the name Theresa Slane, the detective inspector said, "I think, sir, you had better wait for a few minutes. The case was handled by Central. It won't take long to get hold of Superintendent Marker. I happen to know that he's over at Weybridge."

It took forty minutes to bring Superintendent Marker to the station, and by that time Mr. Preece, who had already completed a full day's work, was both hungry and tired.

The superintendent was a huge man with a red face, who looked as if he had been poured into his enormous blue suit and left to set. He, also, was missing his dinner and this may have made him even brusquer than usual.

He said, "I understand you've something to tell us about the Slane case. I was in charge of that case. In fact I still am, so you can tell me about it." As he said this, he signalled to a uniformed police sergeant who had come in behind, and was now seated unobtrusively in the corner with notebook open and pencil poised.

This was so different from the friendly chat which Mr. Preece had visualised, that he hardly knew how to begin. It occurred to him that he ought to establish his own *bona fides* first. He said, "My name is Malcolm Preece. I am a solicitor and—"

"That's all right," said Superintendent Marker. "I've looked you up in the Law List. And got your local particulars from the sergeant here. It's just the information I want."

"It has come to my knowledge," said Mr. Preece, picking his words carefully, "that a document exists in which a local resident confesses that he was responsible for the murder of Mrs. Slane."

"Let's see it."

"I'm afraid I'm not allowed to let you have it. I'm sorry."

"Who wrote it?"

"I can't tell you that."

"How did you get hold of it?"

"That is also confidential."

"You'll have to tell someone, sometime. Why not tell me now?"

"There will be no compulsion on me, at any time, to reveal the source of my information," said Mr. Preece with all the dignity he could muster. "It is privileged, as between solicitor and client."

The superintendent made a noise deep down in his throat. It sounded like the sort of noise a hungry lion might have made if defied by a small Christian.

He said, "This isn't a matter of who owes who tuppence halfpenny. This is murder. If you've really got any information, cough it up quick. If you haven't, let's all go home."

"As to whether this information is privileged, I'd be happy to refer the matter to the Law Society. And may I add that I don't care for your manner."

"I don't give a brass monkey if you like my manner or not," said the superintendent getting up. "You've dragged me out when I was just sitting down to my first hot meal for two days. If you nuts are going to come along with phoney confessions, you might at least have the kindness to do it in office hours."

He signalled to the sergeant, who was grinning broadly. "Come on, son," he said, "let's get home."

Mr. Preece was very angry too. But it occurred to him that he had not fully delivered the message he intended. He said, "Before you go, I might also add that I wonder if you ever found the other glove?"

There was a moment of total silence, and total stillness. Then, without seeming to have moved, Superintendent Marker was back at the table, staring at Mr. Preece, and the sergeant was sitting down again in the corner, pencil poised.

It was as though a film director had said, "Cut. We'll take that scene again." Only this time it wasn't the same scene. The superintendent had lost all trace of fatigue and boredom. He had settled his massive form into his chair, with the air of one who was prepared to stay in it all night.

"Well, Mr.—Mr. Preece," he said, *"what* was that about a glove?"

The next two hours were easily the most unpleasant that Mr. Preece had ever spent. He had never imagined that the same question could be asked, so many times, in so many different ways. At the end of it he was quite surprised to find that it was only nine o'clock. He would not have been greatly surprised if it had been midnight. His housekeeper, Mrs. Biddlecombe, was waiting for him, looking worried.

"I couldn't imagine what had happened to you," she said. "I rang the station. They said your train was on time, and they'd seen you on it. I put your dinner in the oven, but it'll be all dried up."

"I'm sorry," said Mr. Preece. "Serve it up in five minutes."

Then he pushed past the astonished Mrs. Biddlecombe, went into the library, and poured himself out a large whisky.

"It's quite clear," said Mr. Sexton, "that you can't stop now. You've got to let them have the whole story."

"That's quite impossible," said Mr. Preece. He had not slept well, but the coming of morning had restored some of his self-possession. The familiar surroundings of his office had gone a long way to complete the cure.

"Why is it impossible?"

"Because they'll go straight down to the hospital and start questioning Colonel Spender. He's a sick man. If that superintendent starts on *him*, it'll probably kill him."

"It's his own fault. He's brought the whole thing on himself by writing that damn silly note."

"And how are we going to explain to the colonel about opening it?"

Mr. Sexton said, with a touch of impatience, "Tell him the truth. It was a mistake. And a perfectly natural one—"

"I know—but—"

"Have you considered what may happen if you don't come clean?"

"What do you mean? What could happen? They can pester me with a lot of damn silly questions, but they can't arrest me."

"Can't they?"

"What for?"

"For the murder of Theresa Slane."

Mr. Preece stared at him as though he had gone mad.

Mr. Sexton said, "Do you know what you were doing on the evening of March 22nd, two years ago?"

"Of course I don't. But I can soon find out."

Mr. Preece was a methodical man. His working diaries for the last six years were stacked on a shelf behind his desk. "March 22nd? That was a Friday. I'm usually at home on a Friday. On the Thursday, I see I went to the local Law Society dinner. And on the Saturday I was playing bridge. I assume that on the Friday I was at home."

"Alone?"

"Naturally. As soon as Mrs. Biddlecombe has cleared and washed the dinner things and laid my breakfast, she goes home."

111

"Which would be about what time?"

"She's usually away by nine. Why?"

"I've been reading up the case. The medical evidence was that Mrs. Slane died shortly before or shortly after midnight. Her house is about fifteen minutes' walk from yours, through Knap Woods."

"But—you're joking, aren't you? This is a piece of your nonsense, Andrew. What possible motive could I have for killing the woman? I knew her by sight it's true, but I don't think I'd ever spoken to her."

"It was strongly hinted at the inquest that Mrs. Slane was a high-class prostitute. Appointments by telephone. It was also hinted that a lot of her customers were respectable citizens in the neighbourhood, and that she was making quite a bit of money on the side by gentle blackmail. The police were pretty certain that she was killed by one of the customers she'd squeezed too hard, or too often."

"But good heavens, you're not suggesting—"

"*I'm* not suggesting anything. But the police don't know you as well as I do."

"But," said Mr. Preece, "even if—I mean—if there was the slightest simulacrum of truth in this fantastic suggestion, why should I have gone out of my way to call the attention of the police to myself—"

"Their minds work in a peculiar way," said Mr. Sexton. "I'm afraid that the sequence of ideas which may occur to them is this. You read in *The Times* of the death of your neighbour and client, Colonel Spender. He was an obvious candidate for Mrs. Slane's favours. He was a great womaniser and he lived in the neighbourhood, alone, since his wife died, probably no alibi for the night in question. So you – the real murderer – decide to foist it on to him and close the case for ever. You arrive first at the office – which you did, incidentally – type out this confession, on office paper, with an office machine – they'll be able to prove all that easily enough – then go down to the strong-room, and put the 'confession' with the will. Knowing, of course, that we'll have to have it up at once since you're the executor. I mean – it's plausible."

Mr. Preece, whose face had been growing redder and redder, said in a stifled voice, "I think you're right. I'll go round this evening."

"I see," said Superintendent Marker. He said it in a voice so neutral that the words were devoid of meaning. "Was it you, or your partner, who opened this – what did you call it – deed wallet?"

"I think I opened it myself."

"Could you describe it?"

"It's a stout manilla folder." Mr. Preece demonstrated the size with his hands. "We have one for each client. It would have deeds and documents in it, and any will or codicil – important documents we keep under lock and key."

"And when do you suppose this – this other envelope – was put in it?"

"The will was dated almost exactly a year ago. I assume the envelope was put away with it. Clients often put a letter of wishes with their will."

"You assume? You don't remember?"

"I can't say that I definitely remember it. I'm putting documents away every day. The person who certainly *will* remember it is Colonel Spender."

"Yes," said the superintendent. "I expect he might have done. He died this morning."

Whilst Mr. Preece was still gaping at him, he added, "I'll have to take instructions on this. I'd like to ask you not to go away in the meantime."

"What do you mean, go away?"

"Go abroad."

"I've no intention of going abroad," said Mr. Preece, with dignity. "I shall be going up to my office at precisely the usual hour tomorrow."

"That'll be very convenient, sir. For I shall probably be calling on you." The superintendent was as good as his word. He called the next morning, at ten o'clock, bringing the sergeant with him. They faced Mr. Preece and Mr. Sexton across the table on which lay the famous deed wallet.

"So this is the one, is it?" said the superintendent. "Name on the outside. I see. And a number. You keep things in good order in your office, Mr. Preece."

"We have a considerable number of papers to look after."

"Only the important ones, like this, you keep locked up?"

"That is so."

"Where do you keep them?"

"In the strong-room, in the basement."

"And who has the keys?"

"My partner, Mr. Sexton. And myself."

"I see," said the superintendent. He had been fiddling with the string, and now the wallet fell open, and the will in its long legal envelope, and the smaller white envelope both slid out on to the table. The superintendent, who was holding the wallet, gave it a shake. "There's more inside," he said. "What would they be?"

"The deeds of his house at Bramhill, I imagine," said Mr. Sexton. "And there are a couple of Deeds of Covenant in favour of the local hospital, I fancy. Why don't we have a look?"

The superintendent gave the wallet a shake. The first thing which came out with some difficulty was a packet of deeds. Then two separate deeds. Finally, two white envelopes.

"Hello," said Mr. Preece, "What are those?"

Each one had, typed on it, the words, *To be placed with my will and opened only at my death.*

"Good heavens!" said Mr. Preece. "What on earth—?"

"They must have got stuck behind the deeds," said Mr. Sexton. "Shall I . . . ?"

He looked at Mr. Preece, who looked at the superintendent who was watching impassively.

"We might as well," the superintendent said. "Maybe they say he changed his mind and *didn't* do it, after all."

The first note was short. It said, *I should like my Executors to inform the American Ambassador that I shot the President.*

The second was shorter still. It said, *I am Jack the Ripper.*

"Well," said the superintendent. "That's two more mysteries solved, isn't it." The atmosphere seemed suddenly to have got lighter. "I've been making a few enquiries about Colonel Spender. I understand he was a rare old leg-puller. As a matter of fact, we shouldn't have taken a lot of notice of the first note, if it hadn't been for mentioning the glove. That was odd. Because we did find a glove, a single one, under the body. We kept it up our sleeve, as you might say."

"But," said Mr. Sexton, "if you didn't tell anyone – how did Colonel Spender find out about it?"

"We had to institute a lot of enquiries. It was a foreign glove – artificial pigskin, made in Belgium. What happened, I've no doubt, was that someone told someone else – in confidence, of course – and they passed it on. These things get about. You know how it is."

Mr. Preece nodded.

"I'm sorry it's all come to nothing," said the superintendent. "But that's the way with these enquiries. We have to follow up each line until it runs out. Come on, son."

The sergeant got to his feet.

"I'll show you out," said Mr. Sexton.

When they had gone, Mr. Preece sat staring at the little pile of documents on the table in front of him, a frown on his face. He wasn't thinking about the glove. As the superintendent said, these things got out. Women in railway carriages who had aunts who had cooks who were walking out with policemen . . . What was bothering him was the other envelopes. He himself had emptied the deed wallet, right out, and he was perfectly certain that there had been nothing else in it.

However, as he had sometimes remarked to his clients, "If there's a theoretical solution, I can usually work it out. If I'm stuck, Andrew Sexton can often find a practical answer."

Mr. Portway's Practice

I qualified as a solicitor before the war, and in 1937 I bought a share in a small partnership in the City. Then the war came along, and I joined the infantry. I was already thirty-five and it didn't look as if I was going to see much active service, so I cashed in on my knowledge of German and joined the Intelligence Corps. That was fun, too.

When the war finished I got back to London and found our old office bombed and the other partner dead. As far as a legal practice can do, it had disappeared. I got a job without any difficulty in a firm in Bedford Row, but I didn't enjoy it. The work was easy enough but there was no real future in it. So I quit and joined the Legal Branch of Inland Revenue.

This may seem even duller than private practice, but in fact it wasn't. As soon as I had finished the subsidiary training in accountancy that all Revenue Officials have to take, I was invited to join a very select outfit known as I.B.A. or Investigation Branch (Active).

If you ask a Revenue official about I.B.A. he'll tell you it doesn't exist. This may simply mean that he hasn't heard of it. Most ordinary Revenue investigation is done by accountants who examine balance sheets and profit and loss accounts and vouchers and receipts and ask questions and go on asking questions until the truth emerges.

Some cases can't be treated like that. They need active investigation. Someone has got to go and find out the facts. That's where I.B.A. comes in.

It isn't all big cases involving millions of pounds. The Revenue reckons to achieve the best results by making a few shrewd examples in the right places. One of our most spectacular coups was achieved when a member of the department opened a greengrocer's shop in Crouch End – but that's by the way.

When the name of Mr. Portway cropped up in I.B.A. records it was natural that the dossier should get pushed across to me. For Mr. Portway was a solicitor. I can't remember precisely how he first came to our notice. You'd be surprised what casual items can set I.B.A. in motion. A conversation in a railway carriage; a hint from an insurance assessor; a bit of loud-voiced boasting in a pub. We don't go in for phone tapping. It's inefficient, and, from our point of view, quite unnecessary.

The thing about Mr. Portway was simply this. That he seemed to make a very substantial amount of money without working for it.

The first real confirmation came from a disgruntled girl who had been hired to look after his books and fired for inefficiency. Mr. Portway ran a good car, she said. Dressed well. Spent hundreds of pounds at the wine merchant (she'd seen one of his bills) and conducted an old-fashioned one-man practice which, by every law of economics, should have left him broke.

Some days he had no clients at all, she said, and spent the morning in his room reading a book (detective stories chiefly); then took two hours off for lunch, snoozed a little on his return, had a cup of tea, and went home. Other days, a client or two would trickle in. The business was almost entirely buying and selling of houses and leases and mortgages and sale agreements. Mr. Portway did it all himself. He had one girl to do the typing and look after the outer office, and another (our information) to keep the books.

I don't suppose you know anything about solicitors' accounting, and I'm not proposing to give you a dissertation on it, but the fact is that solicitors are bound by very strict rules indeed. Rules imposed by Act of Parliament and jealously enforced by the Law Society. And quite right, too. Solicitors handle a lot of other people's money.

When we'd made a quiet check to see if Mr. Portway had any private means of his own (he hadn't), we decided that this was the sort of case we ought to have a look at. It wasn't difficult. Mr. Portway knew nothing about figures. However small his staff he had to have someone with the rudiments of accountancy, or he couldn't have got through his annual audit. We watched the periodicals until we saw his advertisement, and I applied for the job.

I don't know if there were any other applicants, but I'm sure I was the only one who professed both law and bookkeeping and who was prepared to accept the mouse-like salary that he was offering.

Mr. Portway was a small, round, pink-cheeked, white-haired man. One would have said Pickwickian, except that he didn't wear glasses, nor was there anything in the least owl-like about his face. So far as any comparison suggested itself he looked like a tortoise. It was a sardonic, leathery, indestructible face, with the long upper lip of a philosopher.

He greeted me warmly and showed me my room. The office occupied the ground floor and basement of the house. On the right as you came in, and overlooking the paved courtyard and fountain which is all that remains of the old Lombards Inn, was Mr. Portway's sanctum, a very nice room, on the small side, and made smaller by the rows of bookcases full of bound reports. In fact, the whole suite of offices was tiny, a box-like affair.

I have given you some idea of the scale of things so that you can gather how easy I thought my job was going to be. My guess was that a week would be quite enough for me to detect any funny business that was going on.

I was quite wrong.

A week was enough to convince me that something was wrong. But by the end of a month I hadn't got a step nearer to finding out what it was.

My predecessor hadn't kept the books awfully well, but that was inefficiency, not dishonesty.

I reported my findings to my superiors.

"Mr. Portway," I said, "has a business which appears to produce, in costs, just about enough to pay the salaries of his two assistants, the rent, rates, lighting and other outgoings, and to leave him no personal profit at all. Indeed, in some instances, he has had to make up, from his own pocket, small deficiencies in the office account. Nor does this money come from private means. It is part of my duty as accountant to make Mr. Portway's own private tax returns" —(this, it is fair to him to say, was at his own suggestion)— "and apart from a very small holding in War Stock and occasional casual earnings for articles on wine, on which he is an acknowledged expert, he has – or at least declares – no outside resources at all. Nevertheless, enjoying as he does a 'minus' income, he lives well, appears to deny himself little in the way of comfort. He is not extravagant, but I could not estimate his expenditure on himself at less than two thousand pounds per annum."

My masters found this report so unsatisfactory that I was summoned to an interview. The head of the department at that time, Dai Evans, was a tubby and mercurial Welshman, like Lloyd George without the moustache. He was on Christian name terms with all his staff; but he wasn't a good man to cross.

"Are you asking me to believe in miracles, Michael?" he said. "How can a man have a wallet full of notes to spend on himself each week if he doesn't earn them from somewhere?"

"Perhaps he makes them," I suggested.

Dai elected to take this seriously. "A forger you mean. I wouldn't have thought it likely."

"No," I said. "I didn't quite mean that." (I knew as well as anyone that the skill and organisation, to say nothing of the supplies of special paper, necessary for bank note forgery were far beyond the resources of an ordinary citizen.) "I thought he might have a hoard. Some people do, you know. There's nothing intrinsically illegal in it."

Dai grunted. "Why should he trouble to keep up an office? You say it costs him money. Why wouldn't he shift his hoard to a safe deposit? That way he'd save himself money and work. I don't like it, Michael. We're on to something here, boy. Don't let it go."

So I returned to Lombards Inn, and kept my eyes and ears open. And as the weeks passed the mystery grew more irritating and more insoluble.

I made a careful calculation during the month which ensued. In the course of it Mr. Portway acted in the purchase of one house for

£8,000, and the sale of another at about the same price. He drafted a lease of an office in the City. And fixed up a mortgage for an old lady with a Building Society. The costs he received for these transactions totalled £185. And that was around five pounds less than he paid out, to keep the office going for the same period.

One day, about three o'clock in the afternoon, I took some papers in to him. I found him sitting in the chair beside the fireplace, *The Times* (which he read every day from cover to cover) in one hand, and in the other a glass.

He said, "You find me indulging in my secret vice. I'm one of the old school, who thinks that claret should be drunk after lunch and burgundy after dinner."

I am fond of French wines myself and he must have seen the quick glance I gave at the bottle.

"It's a Pontet Canet," he said. "Of 1943. Certainly the best of the war years, and almost the best Château of that year. You'll find a glass in the filing cabinet."

You can't drink wine standing up. Before I knew what I was doing, we were seated on either side of the fireplace with the bottle between us. After a second glass Mr. Portway fell into a mood of reminiscence. I kept my ears open, of course, for any useful information, but only half of me, at that moment, was playing the spy. The other half was enjoying an excellent claret, and the company of a philosopher.

It appeared that Mr. Portway had come late to the law. He had studied art under Bertalozzi, the great Florentine engraver, and had spent a couple of years in the workshops of Herr Gröener, who specialised in intaglios and metal relief work. He took down from the mantel shelf a beautiful little reproduction in copper of the Papal Colophon which he had made himself. Then the First World War, most of which he had spent in Egypt and Palestine, had disoriented him.

"I felt the need," he said, "of something a little more tangible in my life than the art of metal relievo." He had tried, and failed, to become an architect. And had then chosen law, to oblige an uncle who had no son.

"There have been Portways," he said, "in Lombards Inn for two centuries. I fear I shall be the last."

Then the telephone broke up our talk, and I went back to my room.

As I thought about things that night, I came to the conclusion that Mr. Portway had presented me with the answer to one problem, in the act of setting me another. I was being driven, step by step, to the only logical conclusion. That he had found some method, some perfectly safe and private method, of manufacturing money.

But not forgery, as the word is usually understood. Despite his bland admissions of an engraver's training, the difficulties were too great. Where would he get his paper? And such notes as I had seen did not look in the least like forgeries.

I had come to one other conclusion. The heart of the secret lay in the strong-room. This was the one room that no one but Mr. Portway ever visited; the room of which he alone had the key. Try as I would, I had never even seen inside the door. If he wanted a deed out of it, Mr. Portway would wait until I was at lunch before he went in to fetch it. And he was always last away from the office when we closed.

The door of the strong-room was a heavy, old-fashioned affair, and if you have time to study it, and are patient enough, you can get the measure of any lock in the end. I had twice glimpsed the actual key, too, and that is a great help. It wasn't long before I had equipped myself with keys which I was pretty sure would open the door. The next thing was to find an opportunity to use them.

In the end I hit on quite a simple plan.

At about three o'clock one afternoon, I announced that I had an appointment with the local Inspector of Taxes. I thought it would take an hour or ninety minutes. Would it be all right if I went straight home? Mr. Portway agreed. He was in the middle of drafting a complicated conveyance, and looked safely anchored in his chair.

I went back to my room, picked up my hat, raincoat and briefcase, and tiptoed down to the basement. The secretarial staff were massacring a typewriter in the outer office.

Quietly I opened the door of one of the basement storage rooms; I had used my last few lunch breaks, when I was alone in the office, to construct myself a hideaway, by moving a rampart of deed boxes a couple of feet out from the wall, and building up the top with bundles of old papers. Now I shut the door behind me, and squeezed carefully into my lair. Apart from the fact that the fresh dust I had disturbed made me want to sneeze, it wasn't too bad. Soon the dust particles resettled themselves, and I fell into a state of somnolence.

It was five o'clock before I heard Mr. Portway moving. His footsteps came down the passage outside, and stopped. I heard him open the door of the other strong-room, opposite. A pause. The door shut again. The next moment my door opened and the lights sprung on.

I held my breath. The lights went out and the door shut. I heard the click of the key in the lock. Then the footsteps moved away.

He was certainly thorough. I even heard him look into the lavatory. (My first plan had been to lock myself in it. I was glad now that I had not.) At last the steps moved away upstairs; more pottering about, the big outer door slammed shut, and silence came down like a blanket.

I let it wait for an hour or two. The trouble was the cleaner, an erratic lady called Gertie. She had a key of her own, and sometimes she came in the evening, and sometimes early in the morning. I had studied her movements for several weeks. The latest she had ever left the premises was a quarter to eight at night.

By half past eight I felt it was safe for me to start moving.

The room door presented no difficulties. The lock was on my side, and I simply unscrewed it. The strong-room door was a different matter. I had got what is known in the trade as a set of 'approximates'; which are blank keys of the type and, roughly, the shape to open a given lock. My job was to find the one that worked best, and then file it down and fiddle it until it would open the lock. (You can't do this with a modern lock, which is tooled to a hundredth of an inch, but old locks, which rely on complicated convolutions and strong springs, though they look formidable, are actually much easier.)

By half past ten I heard the sweet click which means success, and I swung the steel door open, turned on the light switch and stepped in.

It was a small vault with walls of whitewashed brick, with a run of wooden shelves round two of the sides, carrying a line of black deed boxes. I didn't waste much time on them. I guessed the sort of things they would contain.

On the left, behind the door, was a table. On the table stood a heavy, brass-bound, teak box; the sort of thing that might have been built to contain a microscope, only larger. It was locked, and this was a small, Bramah-type lock, which none of my implements were really designed to cope with.

I worked for some time at it, but without a lot of hope. The only solution seemed to be to lug the box away with me – it was very heavy, but just portable – and get someone to work on it. I reflected that I should look pretty silly if it did turn out to be a valuable microscope that one of old Portway's clients had left with him for safe keeping.

Then I had an idea. On the shelf inside the door was a small black tin box with 'E. Portway. Personal' painted on the front. It was the sort of thing a careful man might keep his War Savings Certificates and passport in. It too, was locked, but with an ordinary deed box lock, which one of the keys on my ring fitted. I opened it, and, sure enough, lying on top of the stacked papers in it, the first thing that caught my eye was a worn leather keyholder containing a single, brass Bramah key.

I suddenly felt a little breathless. Perhaps the ventilation in that underground room was not all that it should have been. Moving with deliberation I fitted the brass key into the tiny keyhole, pressed home, and twisted. Then I lifted the top of the box. And came face to face with Mr. Portway's secret.

At first sight it was disappointing. It looked like nothing more than a handpress. The sort of thing you use for impressing a company seal, only larger. I lifted it out, picked up a piece of clean white paper off the shelf, slid it in, and pressed down the handle. Then I released it, and extracted the paper.

Imprinted on it was a neat, orange, Revenue Stamp for twenty pounds. I went back to the box. Inside was a tray, and arranged in it stamps of various denominations, starting at ten shillings, one pound, two pounds and five pounds and so on upwards. The largest was for a hundred pounds.

I picked one out and held it up to the light. It was beautifully made. Mr. Portway had not wasted his time at Bertalozzi's Florentine atelier. There was even an arrangement of cogs behind each stamp by which the three figures of the date could be set; tiny, delicate wheels, each a masterpiece of the watchmaker's art.

I heard the footsteps crossing the courtyard, and Mr. Portway was through the door before I even had time to put down the seal I was holding.

"What are you doing here?" I said stupidly.

"When anyone turns on the strong-room light," he said, "it turns on the light in my office, too. I've got a private arrangement with the caretaker of the big block at the end who keeps an eye open for me. If she sees my light on, she telephones me."

"I see," I said. Once I had got over the actual shock of seeing him there, I wasn't alarmed. I was half his age, and twice his size. "I've just been admiring your homework. Every man should have his own stamp office. A lovely piece of work."

"Is it not?" agreed Mr. Portway, blinking up at me under the strong light. I could read in his Chelonian face neither fear nor anger. Rather a sardonic amusement at the turn of affairs. "Are you a private detective, by any chance?"

I told him who I was.

"You have been admiring my little machine?"

"My only real surprise is that no one has thought of it before."

"Yes," he said. "It's very useful. To a practising solicitor, of course. I used to find it a permanent source of irritation that my clients should pay more to the Government – who, after all, hadn't raised a finger to earn it – than they did to me. Do you realise that if I act for the purchase of a London house for £8,000 I get about fifty-five, whilst the Government's share is eighty?"

"Scandalous," I agreed. "And so you devised this little machine to adjust the balance. Such a simple and foolproof form of forgery, when you come to think of it." The more I thought of it the more I liked it. "Just think of the effort you would have to expend – to say nothing of stocks of special paper – if you set out to forge a hundred one pound notes. Whereas with this machine – a small die – a simple pressure."

"Oh, there's more to it than that," said Mr. Portway. "A man would be a fool to forge treasury notes. They have to be passed into circulation, and each one is a potential danger to its maker. Here, when I have stamped a document, it goes into a deed box. It may not be looked at again for twenty years. Possibly never."

"As a professional accountant," I said, "I am not sure that that angle is not the one that appeals to me most. Let me see. Take that purchase you were talking about. Your client would give you two cheques, one for your costs, which goes through the books in the ordinary way, and a separate one for the stamp duty."

"Made out to cash."

"Made out to cash, of course. Which you would yourself cash at the bank. Then come back here—"

"I always took the trouble to walk through the stamp office in case anyone should be watching me."

"Very sound," I said. "Then you came back here, stamped the document yourself that evening, and put the money in your pocket. It never appeared in your books at all."

"That's right," said Mr. Portway. He seemed gratified at the speed with which I had perceived the finer points of his arrangements.

"There's only one thing I can't quite see," I said. "You're a bachelor, a man with simple tastes. Could you not – I don't want to sound pompous – by working a little harder, have made sufficient money legitimately for your reasonable needs?"

Mr. Portway looked at me for a moment, his smile broadening.

"I see," he said, "that you have not had time to examine the rest of my strong-room. My tastes are far from simple, and owing to the scandalous and confiscatory nature of modern taxation—oh, I beg your pardon. I was forgetting for the moment—"

"Don't apologise," I said. "I have often thought the same thing myself. You were speaking of expensive tastes."

Mr. Portway stepped over to a large, drop-fronted deed box,

labelled 'Lord Lampeter's Settled Estate', and unlocked it with a key from a chain. Inside was a rack, and in the rack I counted the dusty ends of two dozen bottles.

"Château Margaux. The 1934 Vintage. I shouldn't say that even now it has reached its peak. Now here" —he unlocked 'The Dean of Melchester. Family Affairs'— "I have a real treasure. A Mouton Rothschild of 1924."

"1924!"

"In Magnums. I know that you appreciate a good wine. Since this may perhaps be our last opportunity—"

"Well—"

Mr. Portway took a corkscrew, a decanter, and two glasses from a small cupboard labelled 'Estate Duty Forms. Miscellaneous', drew the cork of the Mouton Rothschild with care and skill, and decanted it with a steady hand. Then he poured two glasses. We both held it up to the single unshaded light to note the dark, rich, almost black colour, and took our first, ecstatic, mouthful. It went down like oiled silk.

"What did you say you had in the other boxes," I enquired reverently.

"My preference has been for the clarets," said Mr. Portway. "Of course, as I only really started buying in 1945 I have nothing that you could call a museum piece. But I picked up a small lot of 1927 Château Talbot which has to be tasted to be believed. And if a good burgundy was offered, I didn't say no to it." He gestured towards the Marchioness of Gravesend in the corner. "There's a 1937 Romancé Conti—but your glass is empty . . ."

As we finished the Mouton Rothschild in companionable silence I looked at my watch. It was two o'clock in the morning.

"You will scarcely find any transport to get you home now," said Mr. Portway. "Might I suggest that the only thing to follow a fine claret is a noble burgundy."

"Well—" I said.

I was fully aware that I was compromising my official position, but it hardly seemed to matter. Actually I think my mind had long since been made up. As dawn was breaking, and the Romancé Conti was sinking in the bottle, we agreed provisional articles of partnership.

The name of the firm is Portway and Gilbert of 7 Lombards Inn.

If you are thinking, by any chance, of buying a house . . .

Stay of Execution

Number One Court at the Old Bailey was full. And yet at that solemn moment there seemed to be only two people there.

The presiding Judge wore long-sleeved, full skirted, red robes, and a grizzled wig. A deep cleft started from the corner of each nostril, ran out at an angle, and then dropped, so that his mouth lay between goal posts. Over against him, separated by the well of the court, Henry Neville Gordon stood in the dock. He looked baffled. Not fearful, but dumb, and worried, as a man may look when the forces of the world conspire to bludgeon him.

At seventy, Mr. Justice Enright was too old to welcome change. So he signalled to the hovering chaplain to place the black square of silk on his wig. This was optional, but he thought it added an extra solemnity to the moment. He would have preferred the old words, too, now denied to him.

". . . that you be taken from this place to a lawful prison and thence to a place of execution and that you suffer death by hanging . . ."

They were horrible words. But not inappropriate, he thought, for a man found guilty of a horrible crime. A man who had attempted, repeatedly, to seduce a girl, and failing, had shot her, later trying to dispose of body and weapon.

"The sentence of this court," he said, "is that you shall suffer death, in a manner authorised by law."

On the word, the reporters, who had worked their way close to the swing doors, jumped through them and clattered off down the passage to the row of telephone booths. Receivers were off the hook, and their voices were breathing into the mouthpieces, before Harry Gordon had left the dock.

Sentence on Highgate Killer said the posters in blood red, which matched Mr. Justice Enright's robes. *Death* they said. And again, and again, *Death*. The old beast of capital punishment had opened its mouth once more. It had breathed fire from its throat. A man was to be put to death. People could no longer watch it, but they could think about it, they could imagine it, as they made their way home, that evening, to their snug villas and their semi-detached existences.

A few cranks would protest, but not them. No, no. To them the sentence was right and fitting. Harry Gordon was a cold-blooded killer. In a few weeks he, too, would die.

To Harry Gordon himself, the realisation had come slowly; not in one piece, but in several pieces. He was living two lives at once. One in the present, in a brick walled, steel-barred room in Pentonville Prison; the other in the past.

Sometimes it was the distant past. Childhood, with dimly-remembered, conventional, middle-class parents; left-wing friends at London University; his short and undistinguished career as a National Serviceman. The resolve, taken on the top of a bus going west down Kings Road, Chelsea, to become an architect. The fight to qualify, the anti-climax when he had qualified and could get no work. The day he had met Janine.

Like a camera tracking suddenly into a close-up, his mind focused on Janine.

He could remember every detail of the meeting.

In his wanderings round North London he had spotted a tumbledown box of bricks called Sandpit Cottage. His architect's eye had seen possibilities in it, as living quarters, office and studio. He had got hold of the details from the agent, and had hurried down to talk to his solicitor, Mr. Beeding, at his office in New Square.

While he was in the waiting room, Mr. Henry, the old litigation clerk, had poked his head round the door and said, in his rich, comedian's voice, "Come along, come along. You can make yourself useful, Mr. Gordon. There's a signature to be witnessed."

Janine was sitting in a chair beside Mr. Beeding's desk, pen poised.

"Can I start now?" she said. As soon as she spoke, he had recognised her. He had seen her in two plays and half a dozen films. He watched, fascinated, as she wrote her name *Janine Mann*. So that was her real name, as well as her stage name. He and Mr. Henry witnessed the signature. Mr. Beeding introduced him.

"A rising young architect."

"Not true," he had said. "Planning to rise, if you like, but not yet left the runway."

"A lot of people I know," she had given a sideways glance at Mr. Beeding as she spoke, "would be glad to be safe back on the runway."

And that was the beginning of it. How long had it been, after that, before she was first in his arms?

She was ten years older than he was. Away from footlights and camera and make-up artists, she was not particularly beautiful. It was her body which had fascinated him. Like all actresses, models, and courtesans, she was conscious of it, but never self-conscious about it, that extraordinary putting together of flesh and muscle and skin and bone which made her a woman in a thousand.

"I am an architect," he had told her, stroking her bare shoulder. "And I know that what pleases the eye is proportion – and the proper assembly of parts into a whole." And she had laughed at him.

She was always laughing at him. He sometimes wondered why she bothered with him at all. He had no money, and money was one of her preoccupations. She had not been in a big film or a successful play for some time, and he guessed that, like most stage folk, she was finding it hard to pay the tax on the years of success. Probably that accounted for her frequent visits to Mr. Beeding.

May be it was his youth, and his intolerance, that she found refreshing. She liked talking. She would spend long afternoons lying on a sofa in his drawing office (Sandpit Cottage had turned out to be all he hoped); she would talk about life, about plays (with plenty of detail), about men (but with less detail), about religion and politics, hope and fear, life and death.

She had never given him anything. Not her money, nor her body – that sensuous, sensitive body, an artist's pleasure, a sculptor's delight, thrown down like a discarded toy on his shabby sofa; not even when, one afternoon, provoked beyond enduring, he had tried to take it by force, and she had astonished him with the strength in her thin wrists.

But though she would give him nothing, she had borrowed something. Once.

The camera jerked forward again.

She had arrived unusually late, out of the murk and the drizzle of a November night. It must have been nearly eight o'clock when he heard her red Aston Martin draw up, with the distinctive squeal of its unadjusted brakes, in the courtyard behind his house.

The moment she came in, he saw that she was frightened. He tried, for nearly an hour, to find out what was wrong. And all he had learned was that she was meeting a man, later on that evening, at his home, which she would get to by driving down the Great West Road, and that she was frightened of him.

The first part might have been true or untrue. She lied often, and easily. But of the second part, there was no doubt. Her voice said it, her eyes said it, her hands said it.

All the same, he had been surprised at her request.

"I know you've got a revolver somewhere," she said. "You told me you brought one back from Germany. I want to borrow it."

"It's not a revolver," he said, playing for time. "It's an automatic. And it's a dangerous weapon."

"It's got a safety catch – something like that. You could show me how it works. I only want to frighten him."

"Frighten who?"

"I can't tell you."

"If you won't tell me, I won't lend you the gun."

But of course he had, first carefully removing every bullet from the magazine. And just before nine, she had driven away. And five minutes later, he had followed her.

He could pick her up easily enough, even on such a vile night. If she was going down the Great West Road, she would take the North Circular. She had the faster car, but he was the better driver. He picked up the Aston Martin near Ealing, and fell in behind her.

131

He had no firm idea of what he wanted to do. It seemed unlikely that there was anything he could do. But he was infatuated with her. And she was going to meet another man. He had to be there.

At the road junction before London Airport he lost her. He got caught, for a moment, behind a block of airport traffic. She slipped through, and was gone.

It was the worst of all possible places for it to happen. She might have turned right, down the Slough Road, gone straight ahead, to Staines, or even forked left, through Hounslow.

With no clue to help him, he had chosen the middle road. After a couple of miles that, too, forked: left to Laleham and Chertsey, right to Staines.

It was the beginning of an hour of fruitless searching, casting round, questioning pedestrians who, hurrying home, their heads down against the driving rain, had seen no Aston Martin and wouldn't have recognised one if they had – and goodnight to you.

At about half past ten, he had stopped at a big road-house, drunk two double whiskies and eaten a sandwich in the crowded saloon bar. At midnight, with the rain easing up a little as the wind dropped, he had got back to Sandpit Cottage.

The red Aston Martin was standing in the yard. Janine was on the back seat, crouching down, as though hiding from him. He knew she was dead before his hand felt the blood, caked, but still sticky, on the front of her coat. His gun was on the floor of the car.

Why didn't I send for the police at once, he thought. While my car was still warm, and the mud on it was wet, and the road-house might still have had my whisky glass, unwashed-up, with my fingerprints on it, and the girl who served me might still have remembered me, and one of the people I'd stopped – just one of them – might really have remembered it, if asked about it straightaway.

Instead of which, his one idea had been to get rid of everything – body, gun and car. Epping Forest seemed to him to be the best place. In the lonelier parts of the Forest a body might lie undiscovered for weeks, or months; then drive the car back to within a mile or two of Highgate, and walk the rest of the way home. The gun could go down a drain. And the bullets, which he had so carefully removed from the magazine. He must take care not to be seen driving away from the house. He must wear gloves the whole time. He must not lose his head.

It might have worked, too, if, turning off the main road into the Forest, he hadn't bogged the low-slung Aston Martin in a mud patch. And if, while he was accelerating desperately to get out of it, a police car had not slid up behind him, and a maddeningly polite voice enquired, "Can we help you, sir?"

That stout, competent, middle-aged solicitor Alfred Beeding, of Bastwick and Beeding, drove down to Pentonville Prison in a taxi, with Hargest Macrea, Q.C., and Bridget Avery. Mr. Macrea had a long thin face, smiled rarely and enjoyed classical music and the wines of the Médoc. Bridget was pretty and normally laughed a good deal, but that morning she, too, sat under a black cloud.

The silence in the taxi was broken only once, by Macrea, who said suddenly, "If only it had been a fine night. When it's raining people notice nothing, except their wet trouser-legs."

Mr. Beeding nodded. It had been one of the most puzzling things about the case. Gordon swore that he had spoken to at least four pedestrians but, in spite of an appeal splashed in all the newspapers, only Mr. Keun had come forward, and he had been a most unsatisfactory witness, vague about times, uncertain about details, self-contradictory.

At the door of the interview room, Mr. Beeding, noticing Bridget's white face, had said, "If you'd rather not come in, I could manage—"

"I'll be all right," she said in a shaky voice.

"It'll be a great help if you can get down everything he says. Don't worry about Macrea and me. But anything *he* lets drop. Anything at all. It might be useful."

It was a long interview, and Bridget's wrist was aching before it was finished. He talked too fast. It was as if he realised that there was a time limit for talking, as for everything else.

"Slow," she wanted to say. "Go slower. Stop for a moment, stop, and think." But the words came, faster and faster; repeating the story she had heard so many times before, picking it up, putting it down, wringing the last, stale drop of fact out of it.

Mr. Beeding prodded with an occasional question, Macrea sat unmoving, and apparently unmoved.

It was when they rose to go that Harry Gordon looked at Bridget. He seemed to be noticing her for the first time, to be taking in her pleasant face, her white skin under her reddish hair.

She looked at him, too, and saw what lay behind his eyes. She saw that realisation had begun to creep back into him, like feeling into a frozen limb. She saw that he was terrified, and desperate and alone. And she hated herself, and everyone else, bitterly, for what they were doing to him.

"Do you think he's got a chance?" she asked the question as they were driving back, and it was Hargest Macrea who answered, in his dry Lowland voice.

"A lot depends," he said, "on who we get. Some of the younger judges are not too happy about the Homicide Act. It won't affect their legal judgment, of course, but if we could get any new evidence – of any sort – I think they'd be happy to listen to it."

"How long have we got?"

"About three weeks . . ."

At the same moment, two very different men were talking about the case.

Chief Superintendent Lacey, who had a healthy red face and white hair cut very short, was the head of the C.I.D. in No. 3 District. Anderson, the man he was talking to, had the look of a barrister. He had, in fact, abandoned a career at the Bar to come to New Scotland Yard of which he was now the Assistant Commissioner in charge of the C.I.D.

"It was lucky for us," said Lacey, "that none of the three defence witnesses really stood up to cross-examination."

"No," said the Assistant Commissioner. "It doesn't mean, of course, that they weren't telling the truth – to the best of their ability."

"They may have been truthful. They were pretty muddled, though.

And the old girl, I'd say, was definitely cracked."

"Yes." The Assistant Commissioner turned the pages of the report. There had been nothing wrong with the case. Harry Gordon had killed the girl. No doubt about it. And yet standing, as he did, a little further from the case than the superintendent, he had a feeling – something too indefinite to be called doubt – a feeling of a loose end, somewhere, which needed tying up before the case could be docketed and put away.

He said, "The garage hand – Walters – was their best witness. He knew the girl's Aston Martin well, and had serviced it that morning. He had noted the speedo reading on his own service log as 16733. When the car was found in Epping Forest, it showed 16814. Eighty-one miles. It isn't more than ten from Highgate to where Gordon was picked up. How do you account for that?"

"She could have driven it seventy miles that day herself."

"No one remembers her doing it."

"Or the garage hand got it wrong. He could easily have written '33' when it was really '83'. Easy to do."

"He might have done. Garage hands aren't accountants. Then we have André Keun, formerly of Paris, now of Laleham, who says that he was walking home, in the rain, at about ten o'clock when a young man, who might have been the prisoner, driving a car which might have been an Austin, or might have been a Ford, stopped him and asked him if he'd seen a red car. His English wasn't very good, was it?"

"I thought we'd have to bring in an interpreter, sir. Lucky we didn't have to. No one really likes interpreters."

"Finally, there was Miss Huckstep of Muswell Hill, who was passing the north end of Highgate Wood, at a point where the cul-de-sac from Sandpit Cottage runs out into the main road, and saw a sinister man come out of the cul-de-sac, at exactly half past eleven. How did she know it was half past eleven? She heard the church clock strike. How did she know he was sinister? He reminded her of an uncle, a most unpleasant man. He had this same habit of swinging his rolled umbrella from side to side, behind his back – swishing it, as if it was a tail."

"She's quite a local character," said Lacey. "Always bothering the police to give evidence. They know her well down at the station."

"I see," said the Assistant Commissioner. With his barrister's eye he was picturing the three witnesses, estimating the effect they might have had on a jury – Walters: solid, but possibly mistaken. Keun: vague, and a foreigner. Miss Huckstep: if not mad, eccentric.

"It didn't carry a lot of weight against the sort of stuff we could produce," said Lacey. "Those letters – I'd hardly call them love letters. More threats than love. The bullet in the girl's body, fired from his own gun. No doubt about the ballistic evidence. The way he tried to get rid of the body."

"If he was guilty," said the Assistant Commissioner, "it was the only thing he could do. If he was innocent, it was the biggest mistake he ever made."

The words "if he was innocent" hung in the air, twisting round on themselves like cigarette smoke.

"*You* don't think he's innocent, do you, sir?"

"The thing I can't quite fit in," said the Assistant Commissioner, "is the bullets. You found eight of them in his handkerchief drawer, didn't you?"

"That's right, sir."

"And the magazine holds nine."

"That's right."

"So to that extent, it fits in with his story. That he emptied the magazine, and forgot there might be one up the spout. A lot of people who know more about guns than Gordon forget that every year."

"I agree, sir," said Lacey, "but—"

"If he shot her, can you think of any reason why he'd *then* empty the magazine into his handkerchief drawer?"

"To support his story, sir."

"He wasn't thinking about stories – not then. He was going to dump the body, and throw the gun down a drain. Why not take the bullets with him?"

The superintendent shook his head. He wanted to say that there was no accounting for what murderers did. There was often no logic about it. They just lost their heads.

Instead he said, "Do you think he'll appeal?"

"Certainly he'll appeal," said the Assistant Commissioner. "This is one sentence they can't increase."

Macrea knew, almost as soon as he rose, that the Court of Criminal Appeal was against him.

Ranged on the bench, in the most attractive of the many curious Courts in the Royal Courts of Justice, Strand, the burly figure of the Lord Chief Justice looked down at him, flanked on the right by Mr. Justice Jerrold, and on the left by Mr. Justice Rymer.

"Couldn't have been a worse Court," said Macrea to himself. And aloud, "I should now like to draw your Lordships' attention to a passage in the summing up which, it seems to me, seriously mis-states the position as to onus of proof."

The dock was much smaller than the one at the Old Bailey. Harry Gordon's white, tightly clenched face showed just above the edge of the woodwork, and below the iron rail which crowned it. Beside him, on his left, a warder sat on the edge of his chair and tried to take an interest.

Curiously, in this Court, the prisoner seemed much less important. He was a lay figure, propped up in one corner, while the legal argument occupied the centre of the stage.

Admissibility of Evidence, Weight of Evidence, Onus of Proof.

They might, thought Bridget, from her seat on the solicitors' bench, they might have been talking about a bale of hay. Had any of them a single thought for the animal behind the bars?

It was apparent, when the Lord Chief Justice started to sum up in his deep voice, that he was trying his hardest to find some merit in the appeal. He was trying so hard that Macrea made a face, scribbled *Appeal dismissed* on a piece of paper, and handed it back to Mr. Beeding, who looked at it and nodded. Tiny drops of sweat were standing on his forehead. He was not as tough as Macrea.

On the floor below the Court, Mr. Arbuthnot, Q.C., who knew nothing at all of Harry Gordon and his affairs, chose this moment to enter the story.

137

Mr. Arbuthnot was engaged in the case which was due to come on next in the Court of Criminal Appeal. His client, a previously convicted receiver of stolen goods, was waiting, as he knew, in a small room at the foot of the winding stone stairs which lead up to the interior of the dock. He therefore knocked at the door which guarded the foot of the stairs, and peered through the thick glass spy-hole to see if one of the warders had heard him.

At this moment, the Lord Chief Justice, swivelling his bulk round in his seat, and looking directly at the prisoner, had started a sentence with the words, "In all the circumstances, and having regard to every possible contention so ably put forward by Counsel on your behalf, this Court has come to the unanimous conclusion—" when Harry Gordon rose in his chair, hit the sitting warder very hard in the lower part of his stomach, and dived down the winding staircase.

At the foot of the stairs the second warder had the door open, and was explaining to Mr. Arbuthnot, Q.C., that the preceding case would very shortly be concluded.

He was right. Harry, taking the last three stairs with a jump, landed in the middle of his back. The warder fell forward on to his hands and knees, hitting his head against the door post. Harry picked himself up, said, "Excuse me" to the astounded Mr. Arbuthnot, and disappeared in the direction of the Main Hall.

As he did so, an electric alarm bell began to ring . . .

"He did *what*?" said Chief Superintendent Lacey.

The telephone stuttered at him.

"Did you get the entrances sealed? Within thirty or forty seconds? A desperate man can go a long way in forty seconds. Yes, I'm sure you did your best."

In ten minutes, Lacey was listening to the Superintendent of the Royal Courts of Justice, Mr. Breadwell.

"We have to cope with quite a few bad habits," said Breadwell. "Criminals, defaulters, lunatics, all sorts. And we've got quite an efficient alarm system. It's operated by a bell relay. As soon as it starts, Court officials and police officers close all the exits except the front door, and that's guarded. It should be effective well inside sixty seconds."

Lacey considered the matter. He knew exactly where the Court of Appeal stood. There was a long passage, from the point where Gordon had broken out to the Main Hall, and the Main Hall itself was over eighty yards long. Besides which, once in the Main Hall, a fugitive wouldn't want to attract attention to himself by running.

"I think you're right," he said. "He's in the building."

He was right. Harry was still inside the building.

Seeing the officials spring into action at the main doors when the alarm sounded, he had veered off, up a spiral stairway which led off halfway down the left hand side of the hall.

This took him up to the third floor, where he came out into a long, gloomy, but deserted passage. From two storeys below, muffled by the thick walls and floors, the sounds of alarm and pursuit came faintly up.

The passage seemed to be occupied by offices. Harry walked along, slowly. His heart was beating at an alarming rate and he thought, once, that he might be going to pass out. He put a hand on the wall to steady himself, and then moved on.

At the end of the passage was another stairway, leading down, broader than the one he had come up. At the foot of this, voices were shouting orders. The alarm bell had stopped.

Beyond the stairhead, the passage ran on into a dead-end, serving only one room. It must, he thought, be a turret room. If by any chance it was unoccupied he might be able to hide himself away in it. It would, at least, offer a respite.

A notice, painted on the wall outside the door, said DEAD FILES. Harry turned the handle and walked in.

It was an octagonal room, almost full of filing cabinets and cupboards. At a desk in the middle, almost overborne by the forest of surrounding furniture, sat a tall, thin, untidy-looking man with grey hair and thick-lensed glasses.

He looked enquiringly at Harry. Harry, whose mind was on what was happening outside, could think of nothing to say.

There was no doubt about it. There were several sets of feet coming up the stairs, and they sounded heavy.

The thin man rose from his desk, took a couple of steps towards Harry, as if bringing him into focus, and said urgently, "You must be Harry Gordon. I gather that your appeal was unsuccessful."

"I didn't wait to see," said Harry. His mouth was dry, and he could hardly get the words out.

"I suggest you get into that cabinet," said the man. "It's only got my coat in it. And I suggest you get into it pretty damn quickly." It was a long, thin cupboard made of very inferior wood. The door failed to fit by nearly half an inch at the top, and Harry could not only hear, he could see everything that happened. There was a knock, the grey-haired man said, "Come in," in a commendably steady voice, and a police constable entered, followed by a court attendant.

The attendant said, "Oh, Mr. Harbord, there's a man escaped from the L.G.J.'s court. We think he's somewhere in the building."

"I hope he's not dangerous," said Mr. Harbord.

"It's Gordon – appeal for capital murder."

"I remember it. Killed a young woman."

The constable said impatiently, "I take it, sir, you've been in here some little time."

"All morning," said Mr. Harbord.

"Then if you wouldn't mind letting us know if you see anyone – you'll recognise him. He's got a beard."

"If I see anyone with a beard who looks like a murderer," said Mr. Harbord, "I'll shout so loud they'll hear it in the Bear Garden."

The end part of the sentence was said to himself, for the deputation had departed. As soon as the noise of their footsteps had died away Mr. Harbord came across and opened the cupboard door.

"All right for the moment," he said.

"I think," said Harry indistinctly, "bit dizzy. May be going to pass out."

"Hold up," said Mr. Harbord. "We'll find you something better than that."

He got an arm under Harry's shoulders, and half carried him across into the far corner of the room. Here stood a mountainous stack of files. "Have to shift them out a bit. Squat there. Get your head down between your legs."

Five minutes later Harry was under cover. His back was propped against the angle of the wall; he was sitting on a folded garment of thick black silk which Mr. Harbord had produced from a cupboard labelled *Obsolete Forms* and to his right and in front of him rose a protective rampart, five feet high, of what he assumed to be Dead Files. His head stopped swimming and he was reasonably comfortable.

Mr. Harbord did not seem to have a great many visitors. At one o'clock he departed, locking his door, returning an hour later with a paper bag containing a slice of veal and ham pie, three tomatoes, a packet of potato crisps, and a can of beer which he punctured with a paper knife.

"Rough tack," he said, handing it down to Harry, "but it'll keep the wolf from the door."

"I've no complaints," said Harry. He ate every scrap of the food, taking care not to scatter the crumbs about, and finished the can of beer. His appetite had returned.

At about three o'clock the policeman came back. He was alone this time and in less of a hurry.

"Odd sort of set-up you've got here," he observed.

"In what way?" enquired Mr. Harbord politely.

"Ruddy great place, like a castle. Never seen so many passages. Staircases inside one another. Wonder people don't get lost."

"Oh, they do," said Mr. Harbord. "Only the other day the Queen's Bench No. 9 was sitting late, an old lady went to sleep in the public gallery – came out in the dark – wandered for hours. One of the night porters heard her screaming."

"Spooky sort of place," agreed the constable. "I'll be getting on."

"Have you caught your man?"

"If you ask me," said the constable, "he isn't in the building at all. Got out before they shut the doors. Never mind. He won't get far, I promise you."

"I'm sure I hope not," said Mr. Harbord.

Harry found that he was able to listen to all this with detachment. The bulwark of Dead Files gave him a sense of absolute security.

In the latter part of the afternoon he dozed, waking with a start to Mr. Harbord gazing down at him.

"It's half past five," said Mr. Harbord. "In a quarter of an hour I shall be off."

"I don't know how to thank you," said Harry. "Give me five minutes start then follow me out."

"Out?" said Mr. Harbord. "Don't be silly. You'll be picked up before you get past the door." Harry stared at him. "There's only one place in England they won't be looking for you tonight and that's right here."

"But—"

"There'll be a cleaner along between six and seven. She'll be no trouble. Indeed, judging from the amount of cleaning she does, she won't be here more than five minutes. After that your bedroom is entirely at your disposal. There's a washbasin – cold water I'm afraid – and a lavatory along the corridor on the left. I've got hold of those—" he indicated a pair of dusty dark green baize curtains. "Out of Master Sterngold's room – he's on vacation. They're a bit dusty but they'll keep you nice and warm. Tomorrow we'll think about your future. I've got some ideas about that which I'd like to put to you."

Harry said, "Look. So far I haven't dared to ask. But I've got to know. Why are you doing it?"

"The trouble is," said Mr. Harbord, "I'm not sure just at this moment that I'm allowed to tell you anything at all. That's one of the things I'm going to find out tonight. For the moment you'll have to take me on trust."

"All right," said Harry, "I'll do that."

"Sleep well."

When the cleaner had come and gone Harry made up his bed as best he could in the dark and stood for a few moments in the doorway listening to the Royal Courts of Justice composing itself for the night.

Doors were slammed shut, footsteps rattled down stone corridors, bells rang, lifts whined. Gradually, the intervals between such sounds grew longer and longer. Later still he heard the dull thud of heavy doors coming together – safety doors somewhere down in the vaults. Then silence.

It was a silence broken by a multitude of small noises unheard by day. There was a tapping, which he traced to a loose cable in the old-fashioned lift housing. Boards and door frames creaked. Hot water pipes gurgled. As he stood looking down into the darkness of the stairwell, a piece of stone detached itself from the roof above him and landed with a tiny clear tinkle on the tiles three floors below.

The whole building was settling down like a man to sleep. Harry retired to his own narrow couch. The curtains, as Mr. Harbord had said, were dusty, but they were warm. From the Strand, the Court clock boomed out the hours, echoed more faintly by St. Clements Dane and St. Bride's Fleet Street. In a surprisingly short space of time, Harry was fast asleep . . .

Superintendent Lacey got no sleep that night. He sat in the room that had been assigned to him at Scotland Yard. In front of him was the blue-covered file which contained Harry Gordon's private particulars. It was an astonishingly comprehensive dossier. It contained details of his private address, of his club, of every hotel he was known to have stayed at; the addresses of his relatives, friends and acquaintances; his solicitors, accountants, bankers and other professional contacts; of every place to which he might resort for help, for money, for advice, or for somewhere to lay his head. And to all of those places patient men were directed with instructions to enquire and observe. A description and a warning went to all hotels and boarding houses in the metropolis. Railways, coach stations and air terminals were alerted. A special call went out to port and customs authorities, ticket offices and travel agencies.

"There's one advantage of living on an island," said Superintendent Lacey to Sergeant Knight. "It's damnably difficult to get out of. Do you realise that in two world wars only one prisoner has succeeded in doing it?"

"Supposing he doesn't try to escape?"

"If he leaves London we'll pick him up before morning. If he keeps his head and lies low in London it may take longer. May be twenty-four hours. Maybe forty-eight. He's not a professional crook. He's got no contacts."

"I hope you're right, sir," said Sergeant Knight. It was three o'clock in the morning and not the best time for optimism. Outside it started to rain.

At half past eight next day Mr. Harbord entered his room. There were lines of strain on his face but his voice sounded reassuringly level. "I hope you slept well," he said. He didn't look as if he had slept too well himself.

"Wonderfully," said Harry.

"This next bit is going to be a bit tricky. We've got to get you out. I can't see any way round this. We've got to take a chance."

"Look," said Harry, "before we start. I've cleared up all the mess behind there, there's nothing to associate me with this room. If we hit trouble I'm going to run for it, and you're not to get involved."

"Then let's hope we don't hit trouble," said Mr. Harbord. "Follow a few yards behind me and don't hurry."

He led the way along the corridor and down a spiral staircase into the basement. Twice when people approached, Mr. Harbord managed to switch his course into a side passage before any encounter could take place. The basement was a labyrinth without logic or symmetry. Harry soon lost all sense of direction.

"Close up now," said Mr. Harbord. Ahead of them was a small door at the top of half a dozen steps. "It's neck or nothing now."

He opened the door. They were in a back yard filled with coke. There was no one in sight. They crossed the yard, climbed a few more steps, and found themselves in a passageway. At the end of it was a main road, across which they dived into another passageway. At one end of it was a short alley full of small shops. "In here," said Mr. Harbord.

It was a barber's shop. The blinds were down and it appeared to be closed, but Mr. Harbord turned the handle confidently and the door opened. There were three chairs, all empty. A large man with black hair and a flat, white face was standing beside the end one. "Is this the job?" he said.

"This is the job," said Mr. Harbord. "Tom Cox, Harry Gordon."

"Pleased to meet you, Harry," said Mr. Cox. "Hop in that chair." And to Mr. Harbord, "He's all right for height. Bit narrower in the shoulders than I'd been led to expect."

"You can pad them."

"I'll fix them, don't you fuss."

"I'll see you in about an hour's time, then," said Mr. Harbord to Harry.

When he had gone, Tom locked the door.

"Don't open up till half past nine. Should give us time. We'll have that beaver off, for a start. Then give you a nice, close shave. Trim the hair up short. Suntan lotion all over. A military man on leave. That's how I see you."

While Mr. Cox talked, his nimble white fingers were moving.

First he snipped away the trim black beard which had been Harry's pride, and his protest against conformity, for the past three years. Then he shaved him and started on his hair, cutting the sides back, thinning out the top and moving Harry's parting a couple of inches to the left. After that, he got out a bottle which smelled of resin, and dabbed the contents on to the newly bared areas of Harry's face.

"It'll sting you up a bit," said Tom, "but don't worry. You've no idea how smart it makes you look. All handsome men are slightly bronzed this season. While we're waiting for it to dry off, we'll get you togged out."

He opened a cupboard in which a number of suits were arranged on hangers. They were none of them new, but they looked as if they had come from a good tailor. After a critical scrutiny, Mr. Cox selected one of decent, dark grey flannel with a very faint chalk stripe.

"It'll fit you where it touches," he said. "I only got the word late last night, or I'd have found you some more to choose from."

In fact, it was quite a good fit. The coat was the right length, but too ample in the waist. Mr. Cox got out a needle and thread and ran a few stitches into the lining.

"It'll do for today. Get you something a bit better tomorrow. Goes quite well with your brown shoes, which is a bit of luck because shoes mightn't have been so easy. Have to change the tie."

145

"What's wrong with it?"

"A bit Chelsea for the character we had in mind. I got an M.G.C. one for you. Lovely colour – but too risky. Unless you happen to be a member."

"I'm afraid not," said Harry. He settled for a Royal Artillery tie and wandered across to the looking-glass to tie it.

"Good lord!" he said.

"It's the haircut that makes the difference," said Tom. "You'd be surprised. I had a youngster in here the other day. Regular young tearaway. Bow-wave, sideboards, D.A. and all. Wanted a job in a solicitor's office. When I'd finished with him, he might have come straight out of the celestial choir. Got the job, too. You'd better pop out and get breakfast, now. I've got to open up."

Three-quarters of an hour later, fortified by an excellent breakfast, Harry reported back to Dead Files.

Mr. Harbord examined him critically.

"Not bad," he said. "An inch of white handkerchief in the top pocket, and a briefcase."

"Why the briefcase?"

"Most people here carry briefcases," said Mr. Harbord. "You can borrow this one for the time being. Now, let me think. You're a regular soldier, but you're thinking of leaving the army and taking up the law. A surprising number of them do that. You've decided to listen to a few cases in Court. When the Courts shut down at four o'clock, go out and have a good high tea, and come back here as near to half past five as you can make it."

"I'll do that," said Harry, "but on one condition."

Mr. Harbord looked faintly surprised. "Condition?"

"That you tell me why you, and Tom Cox, and other friends of yours, too, I gather, are breaking the law, taking fantastic risks, for a complete stranger."

Mr. Harbord considered the matter. "All right," he said. "I've got permission to tell you a certain amount. Now's as good a time as any. If someone comes in you can be enquiring for a file."

"My aunt," said Harry, "was engaged in litigation twenty years ago.

Her name was Smith." He sat down on the chair beside Mr. Harbord's desk and waited.

"The fact of the matter is," said Mr. Harbord at last, "that you're the King's horse."

"I'm what?"

"The King's horse in the Derby. Do you remember Emily Davison? She threw herself in front of the King's horse in the 1913 Derby, and was killed. That was the moment when people started to take the suffragettes seriously."

"I think I begin to see," said Harry.

"We're all members of a society which has no name, no rules, no officers, and no subscription. And it has only got one object. The abolition of capital punishment. There are a number of reputable and well-known bodies who are campaigning for the same object. We have no connection with any of them. We are unknown, and disreputable. And the difference between us and what I might call the official bodies is a very simple one. We are prepared to break the law. They are not."

Harry said, "It's quite an important distinction, isn't it?"

"It's a vital distinction. No one has ever forced the Government to change its mind without resorting to violence and illegality. Unofficial strikes, public nuisance, assault, boycotting, terrorism."

Harry was fascinated by the gentle but inflexible obstinacy in the face opposite him. Just so, he thought, might an early Christian have looked in the days when Christianity was itself a crime against the State.

"If you've got no central organisation," he said, "how do you function?"

"Mostly we work on our own. Seizing our own opportunities, as they occur. We are, for instance, quite prepared to commit perjury if the need arises. Do you remember the lorry driver who turned up at the last moment and destroyed the Crown case against Annetts? He was a member."

"But if you want help – or guidance?"

"There is a telephone number I can ring. It is manned night and day. And in an extreme emergency there is a man I can see. You won't

147

expect me to tell you his name. I saw him last night. It's with his permission that I've told you as much as I have. He is making arrangements to get you out of the country. There are still one or two places in the globe which haven't signed extradition treaties with us."

"And until then?"

"Until then, we suggest you stay exactly where you are. It is, I think, the very last place that anyone will come looking for you."

"Damn and blast it," said Superintendent Lacey. "He must be *somewhere*".

"Hotel reports negative. Boarding houses ditto. Casualty wards, doss houses, and hospitals ditto. Brothels ditto."

"All right, all right. I've read them. What I want's a suggestion. Not a list of dittos."

Sergeant Knight was on the point of saying, "It isn't my place to make suggestions," but reflected that they had neither of them had any sleep for nearly forty-eight hours, and bit it back. "I think, sir," he said, "that we ought to work on the assumption that he's got out of London."

"Spread the search, you mean?" The superintendent considered. A spread meant involving the Borough and County Forces; and it meant a lot of co-ordination and paperwork. But it also meant that he could go to bed.

"I'm beginning to believe you're right," he said. "If he'd been in London, we'd have him by now. Particularly with his picture in every paper."

"With *and* without beard," said Sergeant Knight. "That was a good idea of yours, sir."

"It'll be a good idea if it works. All right. We'll spread the net . . ."

It is astonishing how quickly the power of routine, even an outlandish routine, will establish itself. Harry left the Court every morning, soon after the doors were opened, slipping out by the Carey Street entrance; was shaved and touched up by Tom Cox, had a leisurely breakfast, and was back in Court by ten o'clock. He spent timeless hours drifting round the corridors resting, from time to time, in the public gallery of one or other of the Courts. He listened to Mr. Justice Neville reading out a long and complicated judgment on the ownership of chattels in transit. He took his midday meal in the dining room on the ground floor which was full of barristers eating mixed grills and reassuring anxious clients. At half past four, he went out and had a large tea. By six, he was tucked into his bed.

This was the part he found most difficult. Mr. Harbord had rearranged the rampart of files so that Harry's hiding place was now entirely roofed over, and proof from all but a very thorough search. The difficulty was that once inside this narrow coffin, he had nothing to do.

On the fourth night, he devised a palliative. There was a five-amp wall socket in the skirting board just outside his hiding place and he plugged one of Mr. Harbord's table lamps into it. A few experiments convinced him that not a glimmer of light could be seen from the outside.

The files which walled him in were arranged alphabetically with their titles towards him. He decided to start with Aarvold *v*. The Random Window Cleaning Company. The file contained what he guessed to be copies of the documents retained by the Court at the conclusion of the case. It started with a *Statement of Claim*.

Harry was fascinated to observe the variety and unexpectedness of matters in which litigants had seen fit to invoke the assistance of the High Court. Neighbours had cut down trees, or refused to cut down trees, had played wirelesses too loud or cards too well, had refused to speak to each other, or spoken all too pointedly.

Towards midnight he had reached Baker *v*. Lovegrove. Mr. Lovegrove had rashly contracted to supply Mr. Baker with as much whisky as he could consume 'until Hell froze'. Finding this an onerous undertaking, the defendant had ingeniously argued that 'Hell' was the name of a pond in his locality. ('Settled on agreed terms', the file concluded.) As he was replacing it, Harry spotted a name which made his heart give a little jump.

'Barker *v*. Mann'.

"Stop imagining things," he said aloud, "it's a common enough name." But it was Janine all right.

She had been sued by Stewart Barker, her agent, for breach of contract, and had counter-claimed to have her agency agreement set aside. The case had lasted five days and she had won.

Two o'clock was booming out from the Strand before Harry laid the papers aside and fell into a troubled sleep.

Next morning, he laid the file on Mr. Harbord's desk.

"I don't remember it, particularly," said Mr. Harbord. "My job's to see they're in order and put them away. What's interesting about it?"

"*Anything* about Janine's past interests me," said Harry. "Because it might lead to the man she was going to visit that night."

"It sounds like a long shot to me," said Mr. Harbord doubtfully. "When did all this happen? Seven years ago?"

"What happened," said Harry, "was that she had a contract with this agent, Stewart Barker. She was a rising young star, then. In fact, she had risen. It was after her first big success. Barker was taking twenty-five per cent of all her earnings. She thought it was too much, and refused to pay him. He sued her for breach of contract. Her defence was that she had actually been under age when she signed the contract, and that Barker had altered the date on it."

"What happened?"

"That's the maddening part about your files. Like a serial. They break off just when things are getting exciting. I know she won. But that's all."

"Her solicitors, I see, were Bastwick, Beeding and Co."

"That's right. It's a one-man show now. Alfred Beeding. He's my solicitor too."

"Is someone taking my boss's name in vain?"

Two heads jerked round. A girl had come into the room. Harry recognised her at once. It was Bridget Avery. And it was perfectly clear that Bridget had recognised him.

For a terrible moment, he thought she was going to scream. Harry measured the distance to the door. He could reach it before she could. He might have to knock her down to gain the necessary start. Not a pleasant thought.

"What are you doing here?" She spoke softly, as if frightened of being overheard. Her eyes shuttled from him to Mr. Harbord. There was no hostility in them. Shock, perhaps, and fear; but fear for him, not for herself. "I thought – why aren't you a long way away?"

Harry was thinking furiously. She wasn't going to give him away. He was certain of that. Perhaps she was on his side. But he mustn't give his friends away.

Mr. Harbord made the decision for him, as calmly as he had taken the one four days earlier.

"It was safer for him to stay here," he said.

"Then you're—?"

"Yes. I'm helping him. Are you going to give us away?"

"As if I would." The scorn in her voice startled Harry.

Mr. Harbord looked at her, shrewdly. "We haven't had time," he said, "to find out who you are."

"I'm Bridget Avery."

"You're Mr. Beeding's secretary, aren't you?" said Harry. "I saw you in Court. And you came, once, with Beeding and Hargest Macrea to see me in Pentonville."

"I was in the whole case, from beginning to end. I've never been more miserable in my life. When you hit that warder and disappeared from the box I nearly stood up and screamed, 'Go on. Go on. Get away, quick.' I didn't think you had half a chance, really."

"I'm not sure I've got more than three-quarters of one now. And anything I have got's due to this gentleman."

"I was originally going to suggest," said Mr. Harbord, "that you went away and forgot all about us. If you work in Mr. Beeding's office, though, I'm not so sure."

"You don't think I'd tell *him*, do you?"

"I'm confident you wouldn't. What I meant was that you might be able to get hold of some information for us." He indicated the open file. "There was a case, about seven years ago, involving the murdered girl, and her agent—"

"A man called Stewart Barker?"

"You remember it?"

"No, but that's the reason I've come to see you." They stared at her. "That's the file I was sent over to find."

There was a long moment of silence in the turret room. Remembering it, later, Harry thought it was like the moment of stillness when the orchestra had finished one theme, and the first soft, enigmatic note is struck which heralds the introduction of a new motif. He realised that something of the utmost importance had been said. The difficulty was grasping it.

"*Who* sent you?"

"Mr. Henry – he's our litigation clerk."

"An elderly man," said Mr. Harbord, "with a face like a clown – an Auguste – the sad one."

"That's him."

"But *why* did he want it?" said Harry.

"Because our file on the case seems to have disappeared."

"Disappeared?"

"I can't understand it. You know how carefully papers are looked after in lawyers' offices. They're all docketed, and indexed, and put away. When Mr. Henry went to look for this one, it wasn't there. It seems someone must have taken it out without recording it and not put it back."

"But why did he want to look at it, particularly?"

"He's been behaving very oddly lately. He keeps talking about Janine. He had some idea that there was a connection between that other case and – and what happened to her."

"And that's why he wanted to look at the old file?"

"That's right."

"And it wasn't there?"

"No."

"Have you any idea who could have taken it?"

"It must have been someone in the office, I should imagine. It could hardly have been a burglar."

"No," said Mr. Harbord. "No, indeed. Most interesting. Mr. Henry, if I remember rightly, is something of a drinker."

"He's been drinking a lot lately."

"Has he indeed?" said Mr. Harbord. "It sounds as if he has something on his mind. I wonder what it could be?"

Harry spent the rest of the morning in Chancery Court No. 2 listening to an interesting case about a disputed will. He was somewhat distracted by the attempts of his neighbour, a middle-aged lady in a daffodil-yellow hat, to draw him into conversation, but he was feeling so cheerful that morning that he was tolerant even of her chatter.

In the luncheon interval Mr. Harbord locked up his office and descended to the buffet.

His first objective was a corner table where he found an untidy, aggressive man with the look of a wire-haired fox terrier, called Mr. Tarragon. Since Mr. Tarragon had a second glass of beer ready on the table, it was clear that he was expecting Mr. Harbord. They talked quietly for some time, Mr. Harbord scribbled an address on a piece of paper, and pushed it across the table. Mr. Tarragon finished his beer and went out.

At the other end of the crowded L-shaped bar, Mr. Henry was standing by himself, drinking whisky. His long, red, heavy face lightened a fraction as he saw Mr. Harbord elbowing his way towards him.

"How are the files, Charlie?"

"They're dead, but they won't lie down," said Mr. Harbord. "What's that? Scotch?"

"With water," said Mr. Henry. "Soda water's too strong for me these days."

"Double Scotch and water, miss."

"You want something out of me," said Mr. Henry. "You've never stood me a double Scotch before."

"I want some advice," said Mr. Harbord. He slid easily into a technical discussion . . .

The wire-haired Mr. Tarragon was plodding up a flight of stairs in a tall building in Denmark Street. The pebble glass door on the third landing said *Stewart Barker, Theatrical and Musical Agent*. Mr. Tarragon knocked and went in. The fat girl wedged behind the desk in the corner said that Mr. Barker was out at lunch. She wasn't sure when he'd be back. He didn't usually get back from lunch before three. Mr. Tarragon said that, in that case, he'd get some lunch himself, and call back, and why didn't they have a lift put in? The fat girl said that it was because the building was due to be pulled down, and as far as she was concerned it couldn't happen too soon.

By a quarter to three the atmosphere in the Law Courts Bar was thick; thick with talk, thick with smoke, thick with the exhalation of alcoholic confidence.

A tear had gathered in the outer corner of Mr. Henry's right eye. Mr. Harbord had watched it filling and swelling. Any moment now, it was going to fall. Any moment now, Mr. Henry was going to talk.

Twice he had come to the brink. There was a heavy weight of unshared secrets in the old man's mind; a load of oppression which it longed to shed, yet dared not; a dammed-up flow of suspicion and guilt, which wanted to burst free, but was held back by a lifetime of professional reticence.

"Time for one more," said Mr. Harbord.

Mr. Henry said, "Look, Charlie. I'm not going back to the office this afternoon. I don't think I could stand it. There's a little place I know round the corner. It's a sort of club."

Mr. Harbord thought quickly. His door was locked. He rarely had visitors in the afternoon. "Fine," he said.

"It was all a long time ago," said Stewart Barker. "And I don't see a lot of point in digging it up again. If that bitch had still been alive I'd have moved heaven and earth to get even with her, but as it is—"

"If you could tell me exactly what happened," said Mr. Tarragon. "I might be able to tell you what use we could make of the information. Until I know that, I'm as much in the dark as you are."

Stewart Barker tried to work this out, but got lost about halfway through it and said, "I'm quite prepared to tell you about it. I've got nothing to be ashamed of. Janine Mann first came to us when she was eighteen. She'd been to drama school, but she hadn't any obvious talent, except a cast-iron determination to get on – which is the only thing that really matters in the long run. I got her a few parts – provincial tours, pier shows in the summer, pantomime in the winter. I doubt if she made two hundred a year the first two years. I took a quarter of it, and was out of pocket by the bargain."

Mr. Tarragon nodded. It wasn't clear to him how Stewart Barker could have twice received fifty pounds and been out of pocket when all he had to do was make a few telephone calls, but he was well aware of the convention that agents lost money promoting hopeful clients.

"Soon after that she got her first chance in the West End. And she took it, with both hands. I grant her that. One thing led to another: stage, films, television. Nothing succeeds like success – in the world of entertainment, anyway. She made a lot of money. And what stuck in her dear little throat was that she had to pay a quarter of it over to me. A month after she came of age, she signed a regular agency contract – as watertight as my lawyers could make it – Duxford and Timmis. I expect you know them?"

Mr. Tarragon smiled thinly and said that he did, indeed, know Messrs. Duxford and Timmis.

"Imagine my surprise when the little so-and-so came along, cool as you like, to my office one morning and said, 'I'm not paying you twenty-five per cent any more, Stewart. You can have ten, or I'll change my agent.' I said, 'you can't do that. I've got a contract.' She said, 'We'll see about that – good morning.' Just like that."

"I imagine you took her to court."

"Certainly I took her to court. I'd got nothing to be ashamed of, had I?"

"And I imagine you won the case."

"Then you imagine wrong," said Mr. Barker. "Her story – or rather her lawyer's story – a man called Beeding was doing the case for her – was that she'd signed the contract before her twenty-first birthday, and I'd put the date in afterwards."

"A bit difficult to prove, surely."

"She proved it, all right. She produced a letter on my office notepaper, signed by me, dated a fortnight before her twenty-first birthday, saying, *Come to my office tomorrow and sign all the papers*. I can't remember the exact wording. That was the effect of it."

"And did you write—?"

"Of course I didn't. If I'd been trying anything like that, do you imagine I'd have written? I'd have rung her up."

Looking at Mr. Barker's shrewd, if slightly close-set eyes, Mr. Tarragon was well able to believe him.

"How did she work it?"

"Pinched a bit of notepaper from my office – she might even have typed it on my girl's machine – she was alone in the outer office for a quarter of an hour one morning. Forged my signature."

"She took a few risks," said Mr. Tarragon. "Did her solicitor accept the letter at its face value?"

Stewart Barker laughed sourly. "Accept it?" he said. "It's my belief old Beeding put her up to it and what she gave *him*, in return for his services, is anyone's guess. It certainly wasn't money . . ."

Harry spent the afternoon in Queen's Bench 3, listening to a personal injury case. He was aggrieved to find that the lady in the daffodil hat had followed him; but his mind was not really on her, or on the case. He was thinking what an extraordinarily nice girl Bridget was.

At six o'clock, Mr. Beeding sat alone in his office in New Square, Lincoln's Inn. He was considering the problem of his litigation clerk, Mr. Henry. First, there was the problem of his drinking, which had grown worse lately. Secondly, there was the question of his unamiability which had developed into definite truculence. Thirdly, and most disturbing, were the hints he had started dropping.

Mr. Beeding was an extremely methodical man. Attention to detail was one of the keys to his success. Planning ahead was another.

A simple solution would be to sack Mr. Henry. But there were arguments against that. To start with he was a very experienced litigation clerk. And if he was sacked, he would start making wild accusations. And however wild an accusation might be, in Mr. Beeding's experience, if it was repeated often enough people would start believing it.

His train of thought was interrupted by the sound of a door slamming, followed by a scuffle of feet down the passage.

Mr. Beeding got up and opened his own door.

"Come in here," he said. "I want to talk to you."

Mr. Henry shambled in and sat down, uninvited, in the chair beside the desk.

"Have you been drinking all afternoon?"

"I've been with an official of the court."

"Drinking?"

"We might have had a drink or two."

"I'm afraid it's got to stop."

Mr. Henry looked at him. The firelight gleamed on Mr. Beeding's round, polished glasses. His face was smooth and composed. The mouth pursed up in a tight smile which hid the teeth. It was a face carefully composed to conceal the thoughts behind it.

"Why the hell should I stop?" said Mr. Henry suddenly. "If I want a drink, I'll have it."

"You can drink yourself to perdition. But you'll do it in your own time. Not in the firm's."

Mr. Henry leaned forward in his chair. He seemed to be trying to penetrate the screen to see what lay behind the rosy light which hid Mr. Beeding's eyes.

He said, "I'll take no orders from you."

"In that case, I presume you'll be leaving us."

"No. You're not sacking me, either."

"Indeed," said Mr. Beeding. "That will produce rather a difficult situation, won't it? Why should I agree to having you here if you're not going to do what you are told?"

"I'll tell you why," said Mr. Henry. "It's because I stayed here late one night, about four months ago."

Mr. Beeding shifted in his chair. If Mr. Henry had chanced to be looking, he could have seen into his eyes, now.

"It's not a thick wall between your room and mine. I heard someone come in through that door," he indicated the private door

157

which led from the office direct to the street. "I wondered who could be visiting you after office hours and I soon found out. She didn't trouble to keep her voice down."

"It was a lady, then?"

"It was Janine Mann. And she was asking for money."

"Indeed," said Mr. Beeding. He had moved again and the red light was back in his eyes. "Indeed. And did I let her have any?"

"Not there and then. You told her to come down that night to your house at Staines. You said you'd let her have two hundred pounds in cash. You told her it'd be the last payment she'd get. And," said Mr. Henry gently, "it *was* the last, wasn't it?"

"I'm not so sure," said Mr. Beeding, "that I understand you."

"You understand me all right," said Mr. Henry. "But if you want it plain, I'll give it to you plain. Janine Mann came in here asking for money and, from what I heard, it wasn't the first time either. You said, 'I haven't got any money here' – which was a bloody lie, because there was nearly seven hundred pounds in there." He indicated the green and gold door of the big wall safe, almost a small strong-room, behind the desk. "I'd put it there myself that morning. However, we'll pass that up. You told her she could have two hundred pounds if she came down to your house that evening, which happens to be the evening she was found, dead, in her car."

"In Harry Gordon's back yard. With a bullet from Gordon's pistol in her."

"Oh, it came out very nice for you in the end."

"It seems to me," said Mr. Beeding, "that you must have been telling yourself some story about all this. Some story which involves me. Suppose you allow me to hear it."

As he spoke, he shifted, very slightly, in his chair. If Mr. Henry had been watching him closely, he might have noticed it. It was the sort of controlled premeditated move which a domestic cat makes as it works into position for the pounce.

Mr. Henry said, "It's plain enough. She had something on you. And it's not hard to guess what it was. Because I've been looking at the Stewart Barker papers. You pinched our office file, but you forgot there's a second set of papers over in the Court. And I was talking to one of their men about it this afternoon. Curious case, wasn't it?"

"I don't remember it particularly. You must remind me."

"She wasn't getting anywhere – not until she produced this letter – on Stewart Barker's notepaper – typed in his office – with what looked like his signature on the bottom of it."

"And are you suggesting that Janine typed that letter herself? And forged his signature? Rather an elaborate plot for a young girl to have thought out, surely."

"I don't suppose she thought it out for herself," said Mr. Henry. "My idea was that *you* put her up to it, and won her case for her, so that you could get – whatever it was you wanted. Which was very nice for you. For a time. Only you hadn't thought things out quite as clearly as she had. Because what you hadn't realised was that it put you in her power, not her in yours. Any time she chose to open her pretty little mouth she could land you up to your neck in the dirt. All she had to say was, 'I was only a girl. He told me what to do. I didn't realise how wrong it was.' People might have been sorry for her – but they wouldn't have been sorry for you. Not on your life, they wouldn't. What a lovely blow-up. What a gorgeous meal for the papers. Middle-aged solicitor seduces girl client. Forgery and fraud. Law Society acts. It'd have been as good as a Cup Final."

"I see. And I shot her, that night, at my house, to prevent her squeezing any further money out of me?"

"That's about it," said Mr. Henry. "It was a bit of luck for you she had her boyfriend's gun with her. Maybe that's what put you in mind to drop her back in his yard. Mind you, I don't expect you to admit any of this."

"Oh, but I do," said Mr. Beeding. "You're absolutely right. That's almost exactly what happened. Except that the actual shooting was an accident. The gun went off when I was trying to get it away from her."

Mr. Henry looked up sharply. He seemed to become aware of the stillness in the office. It was silent in the square outside, too. The last car had driven away; no more voices, no more footsteps on the pavement; a very few scattered lights in the windows opposite. For the first time, the idea of danger penetrated Mr. Henry's drink-dulled brain.

"Why are you telling me this?" He pulled himself out of the chair, and swayed to his feet. Mr. Beeding had moved, too, and was standing beside him.

"I'm telling you," he said, "because I'm sure that you'll respect the confidence."

Mr. Henry said, "Certainly." And it was all that he had time to say, for Mr. Beading's hand whipped round from behind him, grasping a heavy, black cylindrical ruler. He hit Mr. Henry once, on the side of the forehead. The sound was like billiard balls, kissing gently. Mr. Henry folded forward on to his knees.

Moving with surprising speed, Mr. Beeding got round behind the old man and, clasping his arms around his chest, half carried, half dragged him to the tall safe. Holding the limp body in the crook of his left arm, and supporting it with his knee. Mr. Beeding lifted the flaccid right hand and clasped it round the big brass handle. Keeping Mr. Henry's hand carefully under his own, he turned and pulled. The door opened.

There were shelves on each side, stacked with documents, and at the back a number of locked drawers. In the middle there was just enough clear space for a man to stand upright.

Mr. Henry had started groaning softly and shaking his head.

Mr. Beeding hoisted him forward, until his feet were inside the threshold, then he released him, stepped back, and slammed the door shut. Using the ruler, he tapped the brass handle, very gently, until he felt it engage.

"It was horrible," said Bridget. "He was dead. I never liked him, but I was nearly sick when I heard."

They were sitting in Mr. Harbord's room and, Mr. Harbord having departed on one of his rare, official errands, they were alone.

She looked so white and shaken that Harry felt an absurd impulse to stroke her on the side of the neck, as if she had been a frightened horse. He resisted the impulse.

"No wonder it upset you," he said. "Was the safe shut?"

"I don't think so. At least – not properly. They seem to think it was an accident."

"The police think that?"

"Yes. At least, that's what Mr. Beeding told us."

"He did, did he?" said Harry. There was a problem which had to be tackled sooner or later. He said, "Do you think we ought to let Mr. Beeding in on this? He is my solicitor. He ought to be on my side." He could feel her resistance to the idea. "Or don't you think that's a good idea?"

"I don't know," she said unhappily.

"You don't like him, do you?"

"He's all right. He's perfectly easy to work for, I mean."

"He doesn't ask you to take dictation sitting on his knee?"

"Don't be silly."

"The point is," said Harry, "do we trust him, or don't we? You know him a lot better than I do. That's why I'm asking you."

"It's that file. The one that disappeared."

"Do you think Beeding took it?"

"Either it's a coincidence – if so it's a pretty big coincidence—or else, well, I mean—who else could it have been? He and Mr. Henry were the only two people who could have had any interest in it. They were the only two who were in the office when the Stewart Barker case was on. The rest of us are all new. Anyway, why should a typist or a post room boy bother to steal a seven-year-old file?"

As she was talking, Harry was watching her face. He thought, she's got brains as well. She *is* a nice girl.

"It's a thought," he said. "But I don't quite see where it gets us. What you'll have to do is keep your eyes and ears wide open. I'm sure there *is* a connection between the two cases. I've felt it all along. But I'm damned if I can see just what it is."

"According to our pathologist's report," said Superintendent Lacey, "he didn't die of suffocation. He died of shock. If he'd kept his head, there was enough air in the strong-room to have lasted him until morning."

"What a thousand pities," said Mr. Beeding. "Have you any idea how – any further evidence to show what actually happened?"

"He could have come in to put away some papers. The door slammed shut behind him. That could shift the handle. It was only barely engaged. Enough to stop him opening the door, though. You've no idea what time he came back?"

"The whole thing's a mystery," said Mr. Beeding. "He went over to the Courts at about half past eleven. He had an appointment in front of the Master. It shouldn't have taken him more than fifteen minutes. But no one saw him come back to the office. He certainly hadn't got back by the time I left, which was well after six."

"We know how he spent some of that time," said the superintendent. "His stomach was still full of whisky. Did you know that he drank?"

"I'm afraid so. Yes."

"Wasn't it a little dangerous – keeping an employee like that?"

"It's only very recently that it's got bad. As a matter of fact, I'd made my mind up to talk to him about it. Is it important—now?"

"It could have been one of the subsidiary causes of death. If he came in so full of drink he didn't know what he was doing – blundered about in that strong-room . . . There was quite a bruise on his forehead. It looks as if he fell forward – tripped over one of those boxes on the floor, perhaps – and hit his head."

"But surely if—?" Mr. Beeding stopped, got up abruptly and walked across to the window.

"Yes, sir?"

"I was going to say, I don't suppose we shall ever know exactly what happened."

"Probably not," said the superintendent politely.

"By the way," he added, "on quite a different topic. We've found some property of yours. If you'd like to come round to Cannon Row and sign for it you can have it."

"Of mine?"

"Unless there's another Alfred Beeding in the Law List?"

"What sort of property?"

"It's a silver cigarette box. With your name in it. A gift from a grateful client?"

"Good heavens! Where on earth did it turn up?"

"At a pawnbroker's. An honest one, luckily. He was a bit suspicious about the customer who handed it in, along with some other items. Thought he recognised him as a man with a record. So he gave us details of the stuff."

"I'll certainly be glad to get it back."

"Did you report the loss, sir?"

"It disappeared from my desk in this room about a month ago. I didn't wish to cast suspicion on either my staff or my clients, so I kept quiet about it. Not now, Miss Avery. We're busy."

"I'm sorry," said Bridget. "I thought the superintendent had gone."

"I'm just going," said Superintendent Lacey. "And thank you for being so helpful."

"It's a lie," said Bridget. "A complete, absolute, downright lie."

"How do you mean?" asked Mr. Harbord.

"He said that this silver cigarette box was stolen from the desk in his office – and that he didn't say anything about it because he didn't want to upset his staff and his clients. All lies."

Harry said, "Calm down, Bridget. Take a deep breath. Explain."

"First, he never had a silver cigarette box in the office – not in the last two years."

"You're sure?"

"I'm his secretary. I ought to know."

"Right."

"And if he *had* had one, and it *had* been stolen, he'd have raised the roof. Good heavens, I remember about six months ago, when a fiver disappeared from the petty cash float, we practically had to turn our pockets out."

"The important point," said Mr. Harbord, "is not that he's lying. Lots of people do that. The important point is, *why* is he lying?"

"He's worried about something."

"Mr. Henry?"

"No, before that. He's been worried for months. And more than worried. He's scared."

"If we knew what he was scared *of*," said Harry, "I believe we might be getting somewhere."

"He could be telling the truth," said Superintendent Lacey to Anderson, the Assistant Commissioner. "It could all have happened exactly as he said. We've traced Henry's movements. He'd been drinking at the Law Courts Bar at lunchtime, and after that in a private club. He must have had half to three-quarters of a bottle of whisky inside him by the time he got back to the office. He could have wanted to put something away in the safe – he and Beeding both had keys – and the door could have slammed shut. He might have got into a panic and stumbled forward and hit his head. The shock and the blow could easily have stopped his heart."

"Yes?" said the Assistant Commissioner.

"We fingerprinted the safe handle. There are old prints of Beeding's and a thumbprint of his secretary. But quite clearly superimposed on all of them – and obviously the newest – is a perfect set of prints from Henry's right hand. Thumb and all four fingers."

"And yet," said the Assistant Commissioner, "you don't seem very happy about it."

"It was a tiny thing, sir. But it occurred to me that if Henry had gone into the strong-room – either to put something away or take something out – wouldn't he have turned the light on?"

"Is there a light?"

"Oh yes, sir. The switch is just outside the door."

"And the light wasn't on when he was found?"

"Apparently not, sir."

"Someone might have turned it off afterwards. The cleaner?"

"They might," agreed Superintendent Lacey. "And it wasn't really the fact of the light being off that was odd. What was strange was that Beeding suddenly thought of it himself – it was when I was talking about Mr. Henry tripping over something on the floor. He started to say, 'but surely, if the light was on, he'd have seen it?' Something like that, anyway. Then he suddenly changed his mind and turned it, rather clumsily, into something else."

The Assistant Commissioner considered the matter. He respected Lacey's instinct, but it hardly sounded like concrete evidence of wrong-doing.

"Anything on the Harry Gordon case?"

"We've had an enormous number of reports from people who've seen him in different places, from Gretna Green to the Isle of Wight. We check 'em if they look at all promising." The superintendent chuckled. "There's one I meant to show you. It was from a middle-aged lady with a rather eccentric style of writing. Apparently she sat next to him on two occasions in the public gallery of the Law Courts."

The Assistant Commissioner laughed too. "He hasn't got very far, has he then? Could there be any connection?"

"Connection between what, sir?"

"The two cases – Harry Gordon and Mr. Henry."

The superintendent was used to eccentric suggestions from his chief, but he felt that this one went a bit far.

"How could there be, sir?"

"Beeding's a common factor. He was Gordon's solicitor, wasn't he?"

"He was, sir. But even so—"

"I know. It's mad. All the same – would you leave the files on both cases here for an hour. I'll browse through them. Something might strike me."

"I'll have them sent up straightaway," said the superintendent, and made his escape.

Ten minutes later the Assistant Commissioner suddenly stopped turning the papers in the folder which dealt with the death of Mr. Henry. What he was reading was a report from Detective Sergeant Knight, who had been looking into the question of how Mr. Henry had spent the last afternoon of his life. Enquiries had led the sergeant to a senior employee of the Royal Courts of Justice, who had admitted drinking with Mr. Henry both at lunchtime and afterwards in a private club. The employee's name was Harbord.

165

"Harbord," said the Assistant Commissioner softly to himself. "It's not a common name. I'm absolutely certain I've heard it before. But where? And when? And in what connection?"

He was still sitting in the dusk, thinking, when his secretary came in to turn the light on . . .

It was on the following morning, the sixth of his liberty, that Harry had an odd experience. He was walking along a dimly lit corridor on the second storey of the West Wing of the Courts, rendered even dimmer by the fact that a rainstorm was blackening the summer sky outside. He was planning to look in on Appeal Court 3, where an interesting divorce appeal was in its third day.

At the far end of the passage, silhouetted against the light from the stairhead, a man was standing. He was facing away from Harry, and he was holding his umbrella behind his back, swinging it from side to side. The similarity to a squat animal, threshing its tail, was quite remarkable.

He suddenly remembered Miss Huckstep, who had given evidence, though ineffectively, on his behalf. Had she not described to the Court how she had passed the entrance to Sandpit Cottage at eleven o'clock on the fatal night and seen a man − a sinister-looking man − standing there, swinging his umbrella 'like a great tail'?

A conviction gripped him that the murderer of Janine Mann was standing in front of him. As the thought passed through his mind, the man swung on his heel and walked briskly away. Determined not to lose him, Harry broke into a run.

This was a mistake. Startled by the sound of someone running after him, the man swung round.

Harry found himself face to face with Mr. Beeding.

The recognition was immediate, and mutual.

There was an instant in which neither man moved or spoke. Then Harry turned on his heel and ran off in one direction. After a moment's hesitation, Mr. Beeding doubled away in the opposite direction.

"You're sure?" said Superintendent Lacey.

"Absolutely certain. He'd shaved off his beard, and dyed his face brown. And done something to his hair. But it was him, all right. And he recognised me."

"How do you know?"

"How do I know? Because he ran away."

"How long ago was that?"

"Five minutes I'm afraid. Perhaps more. The telephone I went to first was being used. I'm speaking from a box in Carey Street."

"All right," said the superintendent. He spoke on the office line, and two car-loads of men were moving in a matter of seconds. They would be too late. But he couldn't afford to take any chances. Even if they didn't catch Gordon in the Court building, he might be somewhere in the streets outside. He picked up the telephone again, and spoke to 'A' Division headquarters.

Chief Superintendent Mace sounded sceptical.

"If that's right," he said, "he hasn't got very far in six days."

"Exactly what the A.C. said yesterday," said Lacey.

"But I don't think this one's a false alarm. The man who tipped us off was his own solicitor."

"Queer sort of solicitor. Giving away his own client."

The same thought had, in fact, occurred to Lacey. "Perhaps he thought his duty to the public came before his duty to his client."

"It'd be a nice change," said Mace, "if more solicitors thought that. Yes, of course I'll help. I'll put men on to combing all the streets and shops and restaurants in that area. All the same, I don't imagine he'll hang around now."

"We thought that last time," said Lacey. "Remember?"

When he reported the development to the Assistant Commissioner, which he did at the first opportunity, the Assistant Commissioner said, "Ah, that's it," as if an elusive memory had come home to roost. He approved, though absent-mindedly, the precautions which Lacey had taken, and as soon as he had departed, rang the bell for his secretary.

"It was a capital case," he said. "At the Bedfordshire Assizes. Bellamy took it. Almost his last big trial. That would make it 1936, or perhaps early '37." He added certain further details. "See if you can unearth the file. And hurry, there's a good chap . . ."

When Mr. Harbord got back from lunch he found someone waiting outside the locked door of his room. It was a thick-set man, in his middle fifties, with a prow of a nose dominating a strong, clean-shaven face. Mr. Harbord, as he opened the door and ushered him in, thought that the face was familiar to him. A solicitor or a barrister, possibly.

"What can I do for you?" he said. "Do sit down."

"You are Mr. Harbord?"

"Yes."

"Was Charles Harbord your brother?"

Mr. Harbord looked at his visitor in blank astonishment.

"It's an impertinent question, I agree. But the name isn't a very common one."

Mr. Harbord said, "Before I answer any questions at all I should like to know who you are."

"Very reasonable. My name is Anderson. I was junior counsel for the defence in the case in which your brother was convicted of murder. I have never ceased to believe that he was wrongly convicted."

"It's a quarter of a century too late," said Mr. Harbord, "to do anything about it, isn't it?" The words were spoken gently, but there was a hard core to them.

"That's true," agreed his visitor. As he spoke his grey eyes were quartering the room. They lighted on the great stack of files in the corner. Yes. That would be the place. Obvious, if you knew, but an excellent hide-out if you didn't. He added, "But all the same, the lesson I learned there has stood me in good stead since."

Mr. Harbord nodded. He seemed, thought his visitor, perfectly relaxed and absolutely at ease. He wasn't acting, either. Of course he would long since have cleared away any trace of Harry Gordon's presence. There would now be nothing at all to connect him with the matter.

"Particularly," the visitor went on, rising to his feet, "in my present job. I have never allowed myself to feel complacent about a capital conviction. I have never allowed a charge to be preferred unless I was convinced – personally convinced, I mean, not legally – that the man was guilty."

"And were you convinced in the case of Harry Gordon?"

"Yes. I was."

"Are you still?"

"That is a very leading question."

"So long as your mind isn't closed on the subject," said Mr. Harbord. "So long as it's open to honest conviction, then I should say that he still had a chance."

His visitor looked at Mr. Harbord with a smile. What had really amused him was that, in spite of being given two chances to do so, he had not bothered to enquire what job his visitor did. Clearly an unusual man, thought the Assistant Commissioner, as he closed Mr. Harbord's door behind him and walked slowly away down the passage . . .

While a large force of uniformed and plainclothes policemen combed the alleyways and shops between Chancery Lane, High Holborn, Kingsway and the Strand, Harry was ensconced in a barber's chair. When a policeman poked his head in at the door Sam Cox, the owner of the shop, was busily applying lather and addressing the recumbent figure as 'Colonel'. The policeman withdrew.

"I don't suppose they'll bother us again," said Sam. "You can stop in the back room all night if you like."

"No," said Harry. "It's very kind of you. But I'm not risking anyone else's neck for my own. You and Mr. Harbord have helped me enough."

"No risk. Slip the window catch. If they cop you, say you broke in. I don't know anything about it."

"They might fall for it," said Harry. "But I've got a feeling they wouldn't. They'd assume you'd been hiding me for the last six days. And the shaving and the haircut would both point straight to you."

"Have you got anywhere special in mind to go to?"

"Yes. I think I know where I want to go next . . ."

169

Superintendent Lacey was unhappy. He had a feeling that answers to several of the questions which were puzzling him lay close to his hand. And most of them seemed connected, in a curious way, with Mr. Beeding. He had accepted his explanations about the cigarette box, but a further curious fact had now come to light and he felt keen to hear Mr. Beeding's explanation of it.

He found the solicitor behind a desk piled high with papers and files.

"Sorry to disturb you again," he said.

"I'll not pretend I'm glad to see you," said Mr. Beeding. "Without Mr. Henry to help me, I'm getting hopelessly behind."

"This won't take a minute."

"Then if you'll leave us, Miss Avery."

"Don't bother about her," said the superintendent. "There's nothing confidential about this. You remember that cigarette box we recovered through a pawnbroker – a Mr. Samuels. This morning he sent us another item. It had been deposited by the same customer. And it had occurred to him that if one item was stolen this one might be, too."

The superintendent put his hand into his pocket, pulled out a twist of tissue paper, and unscrewed it. A pair of thick gold cuff-links fell on to the desk. Mr. Beeding picked them up.

"Do they mean anything to you, sir?"

"Nice links," said Mr. Beeding. "Solid gold. I'll buy them myself, if they're for sale."

"Then I take it they're not your property?"

"Never seen them before in my life. Why?"

"If you look closely," said the superintendent, "you'll see there's a monogram. Two letters, sort of twisted together. It looks like AB. And seeing that your Christian name's Alfred it did occur to us—"

"Do you think it's AB? It looks like BR to me. Or it might be LR."

"It's not very clear," agreed the superintendent, wrapping up the links and dropping them back in his pocket. "It doesn't signify. We shall locate the owner as soon as we've found out who took them."

"Will you be able to do that?"

"Samuels gave us a good description. In fact, he thought he

recognised the man. That's why he was so careful. A character called Pokey Barret. One leg shorter than the other. Another thing, Pokey's disappeared from his usual haunts lately, which could be connected with a housebreaking at Laleham. If we pick him up for that job we can soon sort out the rest."

As soon as she could get away, Bridget hurried across to the Courts. She told Mr. Harbord what she had heard.

"It stuck out a mile," she said, "that there's something fishy about it. First, Mr. Beeding says the cigarette box was in the office and I know it wasn't. Now he says those cuff-links don't belong to him, and I'm pretty certain I've seen him wearing them. And when the superintendent mentioned Pokey Barret, and the burglary at Laleham – well, you ought to have seen his face."

"Even if you're right," said Mr. Harbord, "what connection has it got with the Harry Gordon case?"

"I thought you'd be able to work that out."

"You flatter me," said Mr. Harbord. "However, I can see one thing quite clearly. If there *is* a connection, only two people are likely to know what it is. Your employer, and Pokey Barret. I don't suppose it's any good asking Mr. Beeding. And Pokey's wanted by the police, and on the run."

"It does seem hopeless," agreed Bridget.

"Not hopeless. Difficult. Our organisation has peculiar but effective methods of getting information, particularly in connection with criminals and legal matters. I shall have to make a telephone call. Not from here. From a public call box." He looked at his watch. "Four o'clock. If the information's available it won't take above an hour or two to collect. The trouble is that I daren't take the return call either here or at my home. I'm under a certain degree of suspicion."

"Under suspicion? How do you know?"

"Immediately after lunch I had a visit from no less a person than the Assistant Commissioner in charge of the C.I.D. His name is Anderson. We had an interesting discussion – about old times."

"It was too late for him to find anything—"

171

"He didn't come to look for things. He came to confirm a private suspicion that this was where Harry Gordon had been hiding. And he confirmed it. He's not a fool."

Bridget said, "I could take the return message. When I stay late at the office, to finish off some work, I get the exchange to leave a line through to my room. I'll do that tonight." She scribbled down the telephone number. "When I've got the reply, I'll meet you – where?"

"Outside the ticket office in Leicester Square Underground Station."

"All right. Then we can think what to do next."

She sounded so forlorn as she said it that Mr. Harbord was impelled to smile. "I've known worse tangles sort themselves out." But not many, he added to himself, as he made his way down to the telephone.

Bridget had no difficulty in persuading Mr. Beeding that she would have to stay late. The events of the last few days had so distracted the office that most of the routine work was behind. At half past five she settled down in her sanctum and started to type out the engrossment of a long lease. Only half her mind was on the keys of the typewriter; the other half was waiting for the telephone to ring, wondering what the message would be, wondering what Harry Gordon was doing.

At six o'clock she heard Mr. Beeding's door slam. At half past six the cleaning woman arrived, poked her head into Bridget's room, and said, "Still here, dearie? I'll do you tomorrow." At seven o'clock the cleaning woman left.

Bridget finished the lease and sewed it up, then knocked off two or three letters which she had in her book. Half past seven boomed out distantly from the Law Courts' clock. Bridget decided to give it five more minutes. The silence in the office was complete.

The shrilling of the telephone made Bridget's heart rocket. She steadied herself and lifted the receiver.

"Beeding's," she said. "It is Mr. Beeding's secretary Miss Avery speaking."

There was a moment's silence, and then a very gentle voice with a slight North Country burr said, "Good evening, Miss Avery. I had a message for you. I'm afraid it'll be a disappointment. Pokey Barret was picked up by the police this afternoon – for a job he did at Laleham. He's being held at Cannon Row police station."

"I see," said Bridget. "Well. Thank you very much."

The voice said, "I'm sorry." There was a click and the line went dead.

As Bridget replaced the receiver, the door opened and Mr. Beeding came in. He seemed to be smiling. "I didn't know that you were interested in Pokey Barret," he said.

"I don't know what you're talking about. That was—"she stopped. No convincing lie came to her.

"I happened to be in my room. I couldn't imagine who could be ringing us up at this time of night, and I was sufficiently curious to lift the receiver."

Bridget said nothing. Her one idea was to get out of the room, out of the office, into the open, where there would be other people. She jumped for the door. Mr. Beeding's hand caught her by the arm, and spun her round.

Bridget opened her mouth to scream, but the sound was still-born.

Harry Gordon had come quietly into the room. He took a couple of steps forward, flung an arm round Mr. Beeding's neck, and dragged him backwards. Mr. Beeding tried, ineffectually to turn. The arm round his neck was throttling him. He gave a choked scream.

Harry dropped his arm and stood back. As Mr. Beeding spun round, Harry hit him. It was a flailing, unscientific blow. It landed flat in the middle of Mr. Beeding's face, knocked his glasses off and sent him spinning. Harry jumped after him and gave him a push. Mr. Beeding tripped over the wastepaper basket and hit his head against the desk.

It was unskilful, undignified and deeply satisfying to Harry, who now picked up Mr. Beeding by the arms and propped him in his chair.

"What are you going to do?" said Bridget.

Mr. Beeding blinked and passed a hand across his eyes. Blood was trickling from one corner of his mouth.

"I'm going to do what I came here for," said Harry. "I'm going to have the truth out of him, if I have to kill him in the process. They can't hang me twice." He turned to Mr. Beeding and slapped him, hard, in the face with his open hand. "It's up to you. Do you tell us the truth, or do I break every bone in your body?"

"Neither," said Superintendent Lacey. He was blocking the doorway, and there were uniformed policemen in the passage.

"It was luck, really," said Lacey. "One of my men happened to see Gordon actually going into Beeding's office. He didn't recognise him, but he didn't think he had any business slipping into the office at that time of night, and told his sergeant – who happened to be talking to me. As soon as I heard it was Beeding's office, I thought we'd better go and investigate."

The Assistant Commissioner said, "Most of our best results are luck. But you have to do the hard work as well."

"What are we going to do now?"

"Legally, it's a bit tricky. The hearing in the Appeal Court wasn't concluded. They'll probably have to start it all over again."

"We'll have two men on the door this time," said Lacey . . .

Mr. Hargest Macrea, Q.C., leaned back in his chair and regarded his visitors with some astonishment. One he recognised as the attractive secretary of Mr. Beeding, Bridget something-or-other. A girl with brains as well as looks. The other, who had introduced himself as Harbord, was apparently an official of the Royal Courts of Justice.

"It's all quite irregular," Mr. Macrea said. "I don't know what my clerk was thinking of, letting you in."

"You must blame me," said Mr. Harbord. "Mr. Tarragon is an old friend of mine. I'm afraid I over-persuaded him."

"Etiquette lays down that I cannot discuss the case with you without a solicitor being present."

"I'm afraid Mr. Beeding isn't feeling very well this morning."

"I read something in the papers. He was assaulted by Gordon, was he not, just before Gordon was apprehended?"

"He was certainly assaulted," said Bridget.

Mr. Macrea looked up sharply. He thought he detected a note of satisfaction in her voice.

Mr. Harbord said, "Could we get over the difficulty by pretending this isn't a conference? All we want to do is to tell you a story. If, when you've heard it, you choose to throw us out, we'll go quietly."

"Well," said Mr. Macrea, "on that understanding . . ."

Mr. Harbord told his story well. He started with the Stewart Barker case. At the end of it Mr. Macrea interrupted him. "Your suggestion is that a respectable solicitor forged an important piece of evidence for a female client, and thereby induced her to become his mistress. But that she turned on him. Why?"

"I should think very likely she got tired of him. And she ran short of money. Those would be two very good reasons."

"And you surmise that the litigation clerk, Mr. Henry, got to know of it?"

"It's a bit more than surmise," said Mr. Harbord. "I spent the afternoon with him. He as good as told me that Mr. Beeding was up to something. He wouldn't say what, but he implied that it was to do with the Harry Gordon case, and that Janine was mixed up in it."

"Drunken ramblings," said Macrea. "Not very reliable evidence."

"All right," said Mr. Harbord. "I agree. But the last thing he said to me was, 'I'm going to have it out with that old so-and-so Beeding. He won't push me around any more.' And he finished up dead, in the safe, in Mr. Beeding's room. Coincidence, I imagine."

Mr. Macrea took a pinch of snuff.

"So now," he said, "we have a solicitor who is not only a forger, a perjurer and a seducer, but also a murderer. And not just a murderer but a double murderer. For I suppose it is part of your story that he was the man Janine was going to see that night – and who shot her with the gun she had so conveniently brought along with her?"

"That's right," said Mr. Harbord. "It's cumulative, of course. One thing led to the other."

"Where does he live, by the way?"

"Staines – on the outskirts. It's a big villa, standing back in its own grounds, about two hundred yards along the Chertsey Road."

Mr. Macrea had extracted a motoring map from the drawers of his desk and was making a few calculations.

"It fits in, roughly, with the mileages," he said. "Twenty-five miles from Highgate via the North Circular. That makes fifty for the return journey. Add a bit for the trip to Epping. Tell me this, when he had abandoned the car in Harry Gordon's yard – *if* he abandoned it, I mean, of course—"

"Of course," said Mr. Harbord.

"How do you suggest he got home?"

"There's no difficulty about that. He would catch the 11.50 from Waterloo to Staines. He'd probably get out at Ashford, so as not to attract attention. He could then walk home, by secondary roads and paths, in under fifty minutes."

Mr. Macrea said, "I'm puzzled, Mr. Harbord. You speak of times and places. How do you know all this?"

"A friend of mine," said Mr. Harbord, "caught the 11.50 last night and got out at Ashford. Eight other people alighted there. He walked to Mr. Beeding's house in forty-eight minutes. And he met nobody at all on the way."

"A very devoted friend."

"Oh, very," said Mr. Harbord. "I've got a number of friends. All happy to work in the cause of justice."

Mr. Macrea looked at him curiously, shifted his gaze to Bridget who was sitting beside him, her eyes alight, and then got abruptly to his feet.

"I want to be careful not to disappoint you," he said. "But I've got to say this. You've just told me a story. It could be true. There's nothing in the facts, so far as I can see, to disprove your version. In one or two particulars it fits in very neatly. But the Crown has got a story, too. And, at the moment, it's their version that holds the field. It convinced a jury at the Old Bailey. And very nearly gained the approval of three judges in the Court of Appeal. Indeed, if Harry Gordon hadn't taken the law into his own hands it would have done so. What are you going to set against it? What concrete evidence have you got – new evidence, that wasn't available before – to make your version more convincing than theirs?" Seeing the look on Bridget's face he added, "I really am sorry to say that, but it's better I should point it out to you now."

Mr. Harbord said, "There is one person who might help us. He's a convicted criminal called Pokey Barret, who comes up tomorrow, morning at the South Thames Stipendiary Magistrates Court for a burglary at Laleham. A burglary which he can't really deny, since most of the proceeds were found under a loose board in his bedroom."

"How—?"

"I can't explain the connection. But it's clear that he had something on Mr. Beeding. At least, that's the only solution I can think of which squares with the facts. He had undoubtedly stolen a silver cigarette box—"

"Which Mr. Beeding says he kept in his office," said Bridget, "but I know he didn't."

"—and a pair of gold cuff-links. And possibly other things as well. Mr. Beeding neither reported their loss to the police nor made any attempt to get them back. When asked, he even went so far as to deny that the cuff-links belonged to him."

"It's odd," said Macrea, rubbing the tip of his index finger down his leathery chin, "but I still don't quite see how it's going to help us."

"It occurred to me that if you offered your services, as Counsel, to Barret – he'd be enormously flattered, of course, to have a famous Q.C. appearing for him – then the police would have to allow you to talk to him. If you could only get out of him what it is he has on Mr. Beeding—"

"The whole suggestion," said Mr. Macrea, "is scandalously irregular. Nevertheless—" He touched his bell and Mr. Tarragon appeared.

"Am I doing anything tomorrow morning, Tarragon?"

Mr. Tarragon said, "Yes, sir. You're appearing for a man called Barret, at the South Thames Court. I've just fixed it with his solicitors."

Late that evening Mr. Harbord was summoned to Macrea's house in St. John's Wood. The Q.C. apologised courteously for dragging him out and offered him a glass of port.

There was a fire of logs in the grate, still necessary on that early summer evening, and Macrea stared for a few moments into its depths before saying: "Well – I've seen Barret. We had a long talk. There's no doubt we're on to something. It's going to be devilish difficult to handle. Legally, one of the trickiest situations I can remember. And I'm not going into it blindfold."

"No," said Mr. Harbord. "What lovely port this is."

"No credit to me. My father laid it down. I just drink it – with reverent appreciation. I want to know where you come into this. And my clerk. He's clearly hand in glove with you. And that girl. The whole story."

"Very well," said Mr. Harbord.

A quarter of an hour later Macrea said, "I've never heard anything like it in my life. I'm half sorry I made you tell me. It makes the thing even more explosive."

"Do you believe," said Mr. Harbord, "that Harry Gordon killed Janine Mann?"

"No," said Macrea. "I don't."

"Do you believe that Beeding did kill her?"

"I'm beginning to think it's very likely he may have done."

"Then your duty in the matter is clear."

Macrea sighed. He reflected that it was a rarity, nowadays, to find a man with clear, hard, uncompromising ideas of right and wrong. Once upon a time there had been more of them about. They had founded empires, started new religions and executed evil kings. He sighed once again.

"It's lucky we've got old Holland sitting tomorrow," he said. "He's pretty broad-minded. I'll have to tell him, in outline, what I plan to do. And we'd better tip off the press. This is a case where publicity is going to be a great help."

Regulars at the South London Court were astounded. Apart from those professionally engaged, the morning attendance rarely exceeded a dozen in the public part of the court, and a couple of reporters. On this particular morning they found some difficulty in getting in at all. Latecomers were actually excluded from the Court.

Those who did get in observed that the press benches were full to overflowing; and that a number of men whom they had never seen before, and who appeared somewhat out of their element in those surroundings, were seated on the benches normally reserved for solicitors and counsel.

"What's it all about?" said Burroughs, of the *Morning News* to his next-door neighbour.

"No idea. We were told there was some tie-up with the Gordon case. Might be nothing in it, but we couldn't risk missing anything."

Burroughs nodded. His dramatic escape and recapture had elevated Harry Gordon into a position above Prime Ministers or pop singers.

"Isn't that old Macrea coming in?"

"That's right. It is. That's Superintendent Lacey – in the bowler hat – and isn't that Beeding – the solicitor? There *is* something in it then."

He gauged with expert eye the distance to the door. If a story really was going to break, he was going to have to get to a telephone.

Mr. Holland came in. The Court rose, and subsided. Mr. Holland, who looked like an intelligent parrot and had a croaking voice to match, said, "I understand, Mr. Macrea, that you have an application to make."

"I'm obliged," said Macrea, climbing to his feet. "I appear for Sidney Arthur Barret, charged with burglary, at Laleham, on March 15th last. Mr. Fellow is with me."

"Yes, Mr. Macrea."

"I have an application to make, and I understand from the clerk that it will be convenient to take it first."

"Certainly, Mr. Macrea. Where is the accused?"

The policeman nearest the door shouted, 'Barret'. The door was opened, and the prisoner came in. He was a scruffy, cheerful, insignificant little man, who appeared gratified by the public attention focused on him. He grinned at a friend in the public benches and was hustled into the dock.

"The position," said Macrea, "is somewhat unusual. I was instructed at a late hour yesterday, and I have only had an opportunity of one conference with my client—"

Mr. Barret smiled in a gratified way. His client !

"Nevertheless, my instructions are quite clear. He has indicated that

179

he is prepared to plead guilty to the offence as charged – on condition that three other offences are taken into consideration at the same time."

"If he wishes to plead guilty the plea should be made to the Assizes, when the case comes up."

"I appreciate that," said Macrea. "But if he withdraws his plea, then preliminary proceedings will have to take place here, will they not?"

"I don't think he can bargain with the Court."

"In the normal way," said Macrea, "I should respectfully agree. The time for considering other offences is after sentence has been passed. But there is a further complication here. One of the offences which my client particularly wishes to have taken into consideration is alleged by the police never to have taken place."

There was a moment's silence. Mr. Holland looked at the police solicitor who half rose to his feet. Before he could speak, Macrea intervened.

"If you would allow me," he said, "to indicate, very briefly, the nature of the dispute between my client and the police—"

For a breathless moment Mr. Holland considered the matter. He knew that what was being suggested was completely irregular – but he also knew Macrea.

He said, "Very well, Mr. Macrea."

"My client," said Macrea, "tells me – indeed he insists – that he carried out a burglary at a dwelling-house outside Staines on the night of November 16th. He is quite clear about the date, which happens to be both his birthday and his wedding anniversary."

"Married twenty-two years," said Barret, "and never a hard word."

"You'll have an opportunity of addressing the Court later," said Mr. Holland. "Go on, Mr. Macrea."

"It also stuck in his memory because the owner of the house, as he found out afterwards, was one of the persons involved – indirectly involved – in the Harry Gordon murder case. A murder alleged to have been committed on November 16th."

The heads on the press benches jerked up, in unison. On the other side of the Court Mr. Beeding turned as red as if a spotlight had opened on him. Then the colour drained slowly out of his face, leaving it whiter than before.

"It was the house of a Mr. Alfred Beeding, the solicitor appearing in that case. My client described to me in some detail how he watched this particular house from nine o'clock onwards. It was not a very comfortable vigil since it was raining hard, but he was afraid to enter the house since Mr. Beeding was apparently entertaining a visitor who, he feared, might emerge at any moment. The visitor's car, a red Aston Martin, was parked outside the front door."

The reporters' pencils squeaked and scurried.

Macrea, who could sense that the sands of Mr. Holland's patience were running out fast, hurried on. "At about a quarter past ten, however, my client saw Mr. Beeding emerge. His visitor – a lady – appeared to be in the last stages of drink, since he had to drag her to the car—"

"Really, Mr. Macrea," said Mr. Holland, "I hardly think this is the time and place—"

Out of the corner of his eye Macrea saw Mr. Beeding get to his feet and push his way to the door. The reporters saw it, too. With one accord they rose to their feet and stampeded towards the exit.

Burroughs had the lead by a short head. He got through the front door of the Court as Mr. Beeding reached his car. He ran across. "Would you care to make any comment?" he said, and this was as far as he got. Mr. Beeding shook him off, jumped into the car and started the engine. The gear lever was rammed home, and the car shot away.

Burroughs scampered to the nearest telephone . . .

"Do you think it was an accident?" said the Assistant Commissioner.

"It's difficult to say," said Lacey. "He was evidently making for his house. By all accounts he was driving much too quickly. It was pouring with rain, and the road was greasy. He couldn't turn the corner just short of his house. Went over the bank, and into the river."

"Yes," said the Assistant Commissioner. He was thinking what a curious part rain had played in the whole story. If it hadn't been a vile night on November 16th, when Harry Gordon started out after

Janine – if he hadn't bogged his car in Epping Forest – if the road outside Mr. Beeding's house hadn't been slippery . . .

"One thing's certain," said the Assistant Commissioner. "No one's going to believe Harry Gordon did it. Not now."

"What puzzles me," said Lacey, "is how they got Pokey to help them. Without him they wouldn't have got far."

"He hadn't much to lose," said the Assistant Commissioner. "The Laleham job was open and shut. He was going down on that for a certainty. And he knew we were on to the others. So it was sensible to bring them in. Of course, he might have had other reasons, too. He might have had strong ethical objections to capital punishment."

One of the difficulties with the A.C., Superintendent Lacey had found, was to know when he was joking. On this occasion he felt quite safe in laughing . . .

The Lord Chief Justice addressed the figure in the dock.

"In all the circumstances," he said, "and having regard to every possible contention so ably put forward by Counsel on your behalf and having considered the new evidence now brought forward—"

Harry glanced at the policeman beside him. He was, he noticed, a particularly large and wide-awake policeman.

"—we have come to the unanimous conclusion that the conviction and sentence in this case cannot stand."

The policeman was grinning.

"We therefore direct that the prisoner be set at liberty. Usher, kindly restrain those people in the public gallery. This is not a theatrical performance."

Outside the door, at the foot of the stairs, Harry found Bridget waiting for him.

MICHAEL GILBERT

CLOSE QUARTERS

An Inspector Hazlerigg mystery

It has been more than a year since Canon Whyte fell 103 feet from the cathedral gallery, yet unease still casts a shadow over the peaceful lives of the Close's inhabitants. In an apparently separate incident, head verger Appledown is being persecuted: a spate of anonymous letters imply that he is inefficient and immoral. When Appledown is found dead, investigations suggest that someone directly connected to the cathedral is responsible, and it is up to Hazlerigg to get to the heart of the corruption.

'…brings crime into a cathedral close. Give it to the vicar, but don't fail to read it first.' – *Daily Express*

THE DOORS OPEN

An Inspector Hazlerigg mystery

One night on a commuter train, Paddy Yeatman-Carter sees a man about to commit suicide. Intervening, he prevents the man from going through with it. However, the very next day the same man is found dead, and Paddy believes the circumstances to be extremely suspicious. Roping in his friend and lawyer, Nap Rumbold, he determines to discover the truth. They become increasingly suspicious of the dead man's employer: the Stalagmite Insurance Company, which appears to hire some very dangerous staff.

'A well-written, cleverly constructed story which combines the unexpected with much suspicion and dirty work.'
– *Birmingham Mail*

MICHAEL GILBERT

THE DUST AND THE HEAT

Oliver Nugent is a young Armoured Corps officer in the year 1945. Taking on a near derelict pharmaceutical firm, he determines to rebuild it and make it a success. He encounters ruthless opposition, and counteracts with some fairly unscrupulous methods of his own. It seems no one is above blackmail and all is deemed fair in big business battles. Then a threat: apparently from German sources it alludes to a time when Oliver was in charge of an SS camp, jeopardizing his company and all that he has worked for.

'Mr Gilbert is a first-rate storyteller.' – *The Guardian*

THE ETRUSCAN NET

Robert Broke runs a small gallery on the Via de Benci and is an authority on Etruscan terracotta. A man who keeps himself to himself, he is the last person to become mixed up in anything risky. But when two men arrive in Florence, Broke's world turns upside down as he becomes involved in a ring of spies, the Mafiosi, and fraud involving Etruscan antiques. When he finds himself in prison on a charge of manslaughter, the net appears to be tightening, and Broke must fight for his innocence and his life.

'Neat plotting, impeccable expertize and the usual shapeliness combine to make this one of Mr Gilbert's best.'
– *The Sunday Times*

MICHAEL GILBERT

FLASH POINT

Will Dylan is an electoral favourite – intelligent, sharp and good-looking, he is the government's new golden boy.

Jonas Killey is a small-time solicitor – single-minded, uncompromising and obsessed, he is hounding Dylan in the hope of bringing him into disrepute.

Believing he has information that can connect Dylan with an illegal procedure during a trade union merger, he starts to spread the word, provoking a top-level fluttering. At the crucial time of a general election, Jonas finds himself pursued by those who are determined to keep him quiet.

'Michael Gilbert tells a story almost better than anyone else.'
– *The Times Literary Supplement*

THE NIGHT OF THE TWELFTH

Two children have been murdered. When a third is discovered – the tortured body of ten-year-old Ted Lister – the Home Counties police are compelled to escalate their search for the killer, and Operation Huntsman is intensified.

Meanwhile, a new master arrives at Trenchard House School. Kenneth Manifold, a man with a penchant for discipline, keeps a close eye on the boys, particularly Jared Sacher, son of the Israeli ambassador...

'One of the best detective writers to appear
since the war.' – BBC

Made in the USA
Middletown, DE
12 August 2018